Praise for
CILLA LEE-JENKINS:
FUTURE AUTHOR EXTRAORDINAIRE

★ "Anyone who spends time with Cilla Lee-Jenkins will look forward to reading her in the future."
—**Booklist**, STARRED REVIEW

"Tan writes in a fun and spunky voice that brings to mind favorite characters such as Junie B. Jones, Ramona Quimby, and Fancy Nancy but is still all her own."
—**School Library Journal**

"Meeting Cilla felt like making a new best friend. I can't wait to share the book with my own daughter."
—**Grace Lin**,
the *New York Times*—bestselling author of Newbery Honor book
Where the Mountain Meets the Moon and National Book Award finalist
When the Sea Turned to Silver

"There's humor and heartache, and future writers of all kinds will see themselves in Cilla. But above all, this is a book just bursting with love."
—**Kate Milford**,
New York Times–bestselling author of *Greenglass House*

"This story has everything: an irresistible voice, a cast of authentic characters, and a hilarious and whip-smart heroine . . . Cilla Lee-Jenkins is brilliant."
—**Kate Beasley**,
author of *Gertie's Leap to Greatness* and *Lions & Liars*

"I challenge anyone to read this book and not fall in love with Cilla Lee-Jenkins. With the spunk of Ivy and Bean and the heart of Ramona Quimby, she's a charmer from start to finish of this laugh-out-loud-funny book."
—**I. W. Gregorio**,
author of *None of the Above*

CILLA
LEE-JENKINS
THIS BOOK
IS A
CLASSIC

Also by Susan Tan

Cilla Lee-Jenkins: Future Author Extraordinaire
Cilla Lee-Jenkins: The Epic Story

BY SUSAN TAN

ILLUSTRATED BY DANA WULFEKOTTE

SQUARE
FISH

Roaring Brook Press
New York

SQUARE
FISH

An imprint of Macmillan Publishing Group, LLC
175 Fifth Avenue, New York, NY 10010
mackids.com

Square Fish and the Square Fish logo are trademarks of Macmillan and are
used by Roaring Brook Press under license from Macmillan.

Our books may be purchased in bulk for promotional, educational,
or business use. Please contact your local bookseller or the Macmillan
Corporate and Premium Sales Department at (800) 221-7945 ext. 5442
or by email at MacmillanSpecialMarkets@macmillan.com.

ISBN 978-1-250-29435-7 (paperback)   ISBN 978-1-62672-554-6 (ebook)
Library of Congress Control Number: 2017944501

Originally published in the United States by Roaring Brook Press
First Square Fish edition, 2019
Book designed by Elizabeth H. Clark
Square Fish logo designed by Filomena Tuosto

3 5 7 9 10 8 6 4

LEXILE: 870L

To my mom, who's there for me always.
And to all the mothers in my life:
Grandmom,
Auntie Esther,
Jenn,
Yvonne,
and Kimmy

CILLA
LEE-JENKINS

THIS BOOK
IS A
CLASSIC

AUTHOR'S NOTE (WHICH IS A FANCY WAY OF SAYING HELLO)

Dear Reader,

Before I start my story, I should tell you that cake is the best.

And there will be *lots* of it in this book.

So get excited.

Because this book is all about my family, and our Traditions, which are rules that everyone knows. They've been around for *forever*, and they have A LOT to do with cake.

So for example, on birthdays it's a Tradition to have cake at parties and to bring cupcakes to your class at school. And it's a Tradition to have moon cakes with lotus or red bean paste inside on Chinese New Year, and chocolate cake whenever my Grandpa Jenkins comes over for dinner (or else he complains). Even Traditions that aren't specifically about cake seem to get there in the end. Like on Thanksgiving, when we eat pie, which you can't convince me isn't just cake with a fancy name.

So, Traditions are great (and delicious), and I'm excited to write a book all about them.

Hopefully you already know me, but if not, that's okay too, and I should introduce myself. My name is Cilla Lee-Jenkins. I'm nine and a half years old. And I'm destined for greatness as a future author extraordinaire.

My last book was (or will be) a bestseller, which is a book that sells the best, and then you're famous, and everyone waves when they see you, and you make lots of new friends. I used to think bestsellers were the best kind of book there is, and the only kind I'd ever want to write.

But this year, in third grade, I learned about a new, better kind of book. (Which is hard to believe, I know, because bestsellers have "best" in their name. But it's true.)

So, I decided to write one.

And, in case you hadn't noticed, this book is a Classic.

A Classic is the most Traditional kind of book there is.

Which means Classics last *forever*.

And everyone knows Classic books, and what they're about, and who their authors are.

Because a Classic is everything a book should be.

Which is a pretty exciting idea.

Luckily, I have the perfect story for my Classic, because my life has had a lot of Classic Themes in it recently, and not just because of all the Traditions (and cake) in my family. Right after we learned about Classics in school, I found out that this summer, my Auntie Eva is getting *married*. And there's nothing more Classic than love, plus Romance sells.

The wedding will also be an Adventure, because Auntie Eva has asked me to be her *flower girl*, which means I'll wear a big, poofy dress and walk down the aisle and throw flower petals in front of ALL our families. This is exciting but also kind of scary, which is pretty much the definition of Adventure (so that's another Classic Theme covered).

The wedding isn't for a while. But I'm sure that between my best friend Colleen; my tablemate Alien-Face McGee (who's an alien disguised as a human, but friendly); my little sister Gwendolyn (who's just starting to crawl and chews on EVERYTHING); and my mom, dad, Grandma, Grandpa, Nai Nai, and Ye Ye (which are Chinese for "Grandma" and "Grandpa"), I'll find LOTS more stories to tell you too. I'm hoping they'll all have Classic Themes, like Quests and Epic Battles and Struggles and Drama and more Adventures.

But at the very least, I can guarantee

you that there'll be lots of cake, because dessert is a BIG Theme in my family.

So, I promise, there's a lot to look forward to.

I hope you enjoy my story, and I hope you can convince your parents to let you eat cake while you read it. (Just tell them that it's a Tradition, so you have to do it. Bonus points if the cake is chocolate or has lotus paste inside.)

Sincerely,
Your friend,
And favorite Classic author,

CILLA LEE-JENKINS
Future Author Extraordinaire

EVEN SQUISHED ORANGES ARE LUCKY

My story starts last weekend on one of my favorite holidays of all time—Chinese New Year.

Chinese New Year is all about Traditions, like eating delicious food, spending time with your family, and getting red-and-gold envelopes from grown-ups with money inside. But most important of all, it's about Traditions that bring you luck for the new year.

Which is why, on the morning of Chinese New Year, I had A LOT to do.

Especially because that day, Auntie Eva was coming to visit.

"Sun nien fai lok! Sun nien fai lok!" I yelled as I danced around the house, helping my mom get ready for Auntie Eva's visit. "That means 'happy new year!' I shouted as I skipped by Gwendolyn's high chair. It was her first Chinese New Year, so I knew it was my job to show her that it's the best holiday ever. I'd been practicing my pronunciation with my Nai Nai because I wanted everything to be PERFECT.

And even though my mom said there wasn't anything for me to do, I was a BIG help anyway. I ran around (and only sometimes bumped into her) to make sure that we were following as many Traditions as possible, to get as much luck as possible.

First, I got dressed in red clothes, which is *very* lucky. I'd wanted to wear my cheongsam, which is a beautiful Chinese dress. Mine is red and gold with pretty buttons at the neck. But my mom said no because it was too cold.

I was disappointed, but then I realized I could get even more luck by wearing every piece of red clothing I own. And I looked GREAT in my red pants, red dress, red polka-dot skirt over that, red sweater, red T-shirt, red headband, and red galoshes with ladybugs on them. Plus I was DEFINITELY warm enough, so even though my mom sighed when she saw me, she didn't make me change.

Then I made sure to find all of Gwendolyn's red clothes, because I'm a Good Big Sister that way. "You're going to love today," I told her as I helped her into red-striped pajamas, red socks, a red T-shirt, a red sweater, and a sparkly red *tutu*. "We're going to Chinatown, and there's going to be a parade, and dragons, and the BEST food!"

"Bah!" Gwen said, clapping her hands, which meant she was definitely excited about it all (especially the excellent good-luck outfit I'd found for her). And she loved it when, as a finishing touch, I found a red scrunchie for her favorite toy, which is an old plush Batman doll that my dad used to keep in his study. (Because even superheroes need luck.)

For my next job, I grabbed all the oranges from the kitchen and set out to put them all over the house. Oranges also bring luck on Chinese New Year, which makes sense because they're delicious.

Nai Nai usually keeps her oranges in a bowl on the dining room table, but I wanted to spread our luck everywhere. So, I put one orange in the silverware drawer, one on top of the TV, two in the bathroom sink, one on Auntie Eva's pillow, two underneath my parents' pillows (as a surprise, for later), one in Gwendolyn's toy box, one in her sock drawer, and one on my mom's desk. I was just about to ask if we could go to the store to get more oranges when I heard the doorbell.

"Who are you?!" my dad yelled out, in his I'm-joking voice.

So I ran to the door, yelling, "Auntie Eva!"

"Cilla!" Auntie Eva picked me up and spun me around.

"Eva!" my mom said, coming to join in our hug.

"Ba ba ga!" Gwendolyn also threw her hands out for a hug, beaming.

And then my dad joined in too.

Because everyone loves when Auntie Eva comes to stay.

Auntie Eva is my dad's younger sister. She's great at drawing, she's AMAZING at playing finger puppets, *and* she's a big fan of Selena Moon (which is my FAVORITE book series and possibly the best series of all time).

Sometimes we don't see her for a while, because Auntie Eva travels a lot for her job. She's been all over the world. But she always thinks of us, no matter where she goes, and she sends me pictures of the zoos or aquariums or museums she gets to visit on her trips. And whenever Auntie Eva's here, she always sits with me before bed and braids my hair while we talk. It's our special Tradition.

When Auntie Eva visits, she stays in my room, and my dad makes me a mini-tent in the living room. So after the hugging, there was lots of bring-ing suitcases upstairs and rushing to pick up the clothes I'd accidentally (maybe) thrown all over when I was looking for red things.

By the time everything was away and cleaned, my mom looked at her watch and said, "Wait, what time is the parade?!" So then there was even more rushing and running. But finally we piled into the car and sped off to celebrate Chinese New Year.

Chinatown was *beautiful*, and more crowded than I've ever seen it. Red and gold streamers dan-gled from windows and in between buildings. And all around, carts sold hot food and pastries, and the air was filled with happy voices and good smells.

Above us, flags with pictures of dogs hung from streetlights, because this is the Year of the Dog. Everyone is born into an animal year, and some of them are REALLY exciting, like the Year of the Dragon. I'm the Year of the Rat, which I used to be unhappy about (because rats are gross). But then

Nai Nai told me that the Year of the Rat means I'm creative and smart, which is good news for my writing, so I felt better. (Plus I like mice, which are almost like rats, and I love cheese, so it all works out.)

We walked through the crowded streets until we finally found Nai Nai and Ye Ye in front of their favorite grocery store.

"Ye Ye!" I ran to meet him. "Sun nien fai lok!"

"Wah!" Ye Ye said. This is a Chinese way of saying "wow!" or "amazing!" or "oh my goodness gracious me!" (which is something my Grandma Jenkins says when she's really surprised). The way Ye Ye said it meant he was VERY impressed. "Sun nien fai lok, Cilla!" he said, spinning me around in a hug (which as you've maybe guessed, is another family Tradition). Then Nai Nai and Ye Ye hugged Auntie Eva (though she's too tall for spinning).

We lined up on the sidewalk for the parade, and Auntie Eva started telling us about her last business trip, and how she visited a fancy aquarium where she got to *pet* stingrays on her day off.

"Wah, so many trips." Nai Nai shook her head (she didn't seem to hear the important part about the stingrays—I made a note to tell her later). "Don't forget to be home, spend time with Paul," Nai Nai said.

"*Mom*." Auntie Eva half-sighed, half-laughed.

"Does he mind that you travel so much?" Nai Nai asked.

"He knows my job is important to me," Auntie Eva said with a smaller sigh. "Besides, he's used to it. His family is really impressive and high-powered. They travel for work all the time."

"Hmm." Nai Nai sniffed. "Not good, all this travel," she said.

"But, Nai Nai, you were excited when Dad got to go on a business trip," I pointed out, confused. "You said it was good because he was moving up in the company."

My dad snorted, and Auntie Eva grinned.

"Well . . ." Nai Nai looked off to the side, like I do when I'm thinking (or trying not to get in trouble).

"So." My mom clapped her hands. "Where are we eating after the parade?"

This is something called Changing the Subject, but I didn't mind. Because just then, Auntie Eva took me to buy a moon cake. (See what I mean about Traditions? They always come back to cake in the end.)

Moon cakes are small and round with beautiful designs on top. Their outsides are thick and golden, and they're filled with sweet paste and a salty egg. Auntie Eva and I split a lotus paste cake, which is our favorite, and she let me have the half with more yolk (which is one of the nicest things you can do for someone else).

We rushed back when we heard the popping of tiny firecrackers and the sound of drums, and Ye Ye swung me up on his shoulders so I could see above the crowd as the parade came toward us.

From where I sat on my Ye Ye's shoulders, I could see my mom and dad holding hands. And I watched as Nai Nai put her arm around Auntie Eva and Auntie Eva rested her head on Nai Nai's shoulder, all the sighing conversations forgotten. The red and gold banners fluttered in the wind, and my dad bounced Gwendolyn, and I was very, very happy because I love Chinatown. All around me were people I know and places I like to visit, and I could smell my favorite foods and see the store windows full of bright cloth and shimmering fans. The egg inside my moon cake was salty and delicious, and when I accidentally dropped some of the yolk onto Ye Ye's head, it smeared into the hair gel he wears and you could barely tell it was there.

And I could see all the Traditional things that my Nai Nai had taught me, and I said, "Mom, do you see that? They're putting oranges in front of the store for good luck!"

Nai Nai smiled up at me, and I smiled down at her.

And I knew she was proud of me.

The music got louder and dancers came down the street, then big lion puppets that wobbled their heads and did silly things that made Gwendolyn giggle. Finally, and best of all, came the GIANT, glittering dancing dragon, swooping and diving. I clapped, my family cheered, and Gwendolyn let out a happy yell, and the head came *right up to us* and *bowed*.

After the parade, we made our way toward the restaurant for our Chinese New Year dinner. There were people EVERYWHERE, and lots of them knew Nai Nai and Ye Ye, which meant we had to stop every few steps to say hello (which is another big Tradition in Chinatown). I call any friends of my Nai Nai and Ye Ye "Auntie" and "Uncle," even though they're not, because it's just another Chinese Tradition. So there was a lot of stopping and hugging and saying "Auntie Stella!" and "Uncle

Gerard!" and getting hugs and wishing sun nien fai lok.

But this takes a while, and Gwendolyn was Fussing, so my mom took us ahead to the restaurant.

My mom was bouncing Gwendolyn and saying "Shhh" and I was making faces in the big glittery mirror on one wall when I noticed that a waiter was setting the table around us. And by our plates, he'd given us all forks.

I looked at my mom, but she wasn't paying attention (mostly because Gwendolyn had grabbed her hair and wouldn't let go).

"Excuse me," I said, in a quiet voice, which happens when I have to talk to strangers. "We don't need forks. Can we have chopsticks, please?" I asked, looking at the pile of chopsticks in his hand.

But the waiter just gave me a funny look. Like he maybe didn't believe me.

Which was strange.

But then the door of the restaurant opened, and the rest of my family walked in.

The waiter said something to Nai Nai in Chinese. She said something back, and then he gave us chopsticks very quickly.

Nai Nai sat down and patted my hand and kept talking.

And I patted her hand back because I was happy to see her.

We ordered LOTS of food—dumplings, and soup made with seaweed, and rice cakes, and noodles, and fish.

"Why do we get the noodles?" my mom asked after we'd ordered.

"It's a Tradition," I explained. "The noodles are long for long life."

"Ah." My mom smiled. "Thank you, Cilla."

"Cilla's an expert on Chinese Traditions," my dad said to Auntie Eva.

"I can tell." She smiled. "An expert with a

creative flair. I loved the orange on my pillow, but the ones in the sink were the best."

"Wait, oranges in the sink?" my mom asked, raising her eyebrow.

"It's a Tradition?" I said, trying to give her my biggest smile. She wasn't impressed.

But the luck from the oranges was already starting to work. Because before I could get in trouble, Auntie Eva interrupted us.

"Well, now that we're all together, I have some news for all of you."

She paused to create Suspense, which is a GREAT storytelling strategy.

"Paul and I are engaged!" she said finally.

"What news!" Ye Ye said, giving her a giant hug.

"Congratulations, Evie!" my dad said.

"How wonderful!" my mom said.

"AMAZING!!!" I said. Then, "What's 'engaged'?"

"Wah!" Nai Nai said. Which seemed to be all she could say for the moment, and she wiped her eyes with a napkin and gave Auntie Eva a BIG hug.

And Gwendolyn was excited because everyone else was excited, and said, "Ba ba ga ba!"

My mom explained that being engaged meant that Auntie Eva was getting married. Then Auntie Eva showed us a picture of her and Paul on the hike where he'd proposed, and he looked very nice and friendly, with the same straight black Chinese hair my dad and his family have and a big, happy smile. Nai Nai and Ye Ye have met him (and LOVE him), but I haven't, and neither has my dad or mom. I was going to ask if we'd get to meet him before the wedding, but then I got distracted when Auntie Eva asked if I'd be her flower girl, and I bounced up and down and said, "Yes!"

There was lots of laughing and hugging after that, and we did cheers, which is when you clink your glasses together. Gwendolyn banged her bottle on her high chair until I clinked it with my cup. And everyone was very happy.

A little later, Nai Nai and Ye Ye and Auntie Eva went to tell Uncle Gerard and Auntie Stella, who were sitting a few tables away. "We don't have a date yet," Auntie Eva said as they came back. "But I told them it'll be July."

"Will Nai Nai and Ye Ye's friends be there?" I asked, turning to my dad.

"Well, they knew Eva when she was little," my dad said. "But yes, usually, at Chinese weddings, you invite lots of people, so parents' friends come too. Not to mention the extended family, like your E-Pah and E-Gung."

"Great!" I said. "E-Pah" and "E-Gung" are the Chinese words for "Great-Aunt" and "Great-Uncle." E-Pah paints beautiful pictures, and E-Gung plays the saxophone. So even though they don't speak much English, we have fun together. (Though they sometimes forget that I don't speak Chinese, and then they sit and hold my hand and talk to me in Chinese. So I smile and nod and hold their hands back, and everyone seems to have a good time, so it all works out.)

"What else happens at a Chinese wedding?" I asked.

"Oh, just some Traditional things," Auntie Eva said. "Like a banquet."

"Ah," I said. "I LOVE those."

"Exactly!" my dad said. "It'll all be really fun."

"Great!" I clapped my hands. Banquets are big, fancy Chinese dinners with SO MUCH food, which I know from Gwendolyn's one-month party (it's another Chinese Tradition, and it's even better than a birthday party, if you can believe it).

"Have you met Paul's family?" my mom asked.

"Yes, they're lovely," Auntie Eva said. "Here, I have a photo of us."

She brought it up on her phone. "This is his extended family—we're at one of my favorite restaurants."

I looked down at the picture, and I understood what she'd meant about Paul's family being Impressive and High-Powered.

In the photo, Auntie Eva sat with a big family in a Chinese restaurant, at a round table just like ours. Paul's mom, dad, and brothers had straight black hair that was perfectly brushed, and Paul's mom had her arm around Auntie Eva and was wearing a glittery black jacket and silver shadow on her eyes. Next to her, a boy my age wore a jacket like the kind Grandpa Jenkins wears with his suits (which is VERY fancy). His hair was slicked back and all in place, and by his plate (and by each of the plates) was a pair of silver chopsticks, laid out in a perfect straight line.

"Wow, what a beautiful family!" my mom said.

"Yeah . . ." I tried to give a small smile and handed her the phone.

And as the adults started talking, I tried to lay my chopsticks out in a perfect straight line on the napkin next to me. Just like theirs.

But that wasn't working, plus Gwendolyn thought this was a game and tried to grab them. So I stuck them in my rice bowl, away from her.

"Ay yah," Nai Nai said. "Bad luck, Cilla." She

reached across the table and took my chopsticks out of the bowl.

"Huh?" I asked.

She patted my hand. "An old Chinese custom," she said nicely. "Just keep them on the table."

"It's an old superstition, Mom." Auntie Eva shook her head. "You can do whatever you want with your chopsticks, Cilla."

Nai Nai didn't take her hand away from mine, but she put her lips together like she didn't agree.

"So," my mom cut in, "do you have any idea what you'll do for the wedding?"

"Yeah." My dad nodded. "You'll probably have a tea ceremony, right?"

"Yes." Auntie Eva smiled. "We'll definitely do that. Though I'm not so sure about—"

Then they started talking about ceremonies, using Chinese words that I didn't know.

I wanted to ask what these Traditions were, because being Chinese means that I should know all these things. But there are SO MANY to keep track of. And I wasn't sure if I was supposed to know them already, and if Nai Nai would be disappointed if I asked, and how many more there'd be. And I didn't want to do something wrong again. But just then—

"Tzuck sang," Nai Nai said as the waiter arrived with a dish of steaming-hot green and brown vegetables. "Tzuck sang" is Chinese for "bamboo hearts," and it's my favorite food and my Nai Nai's favorite food, which is a great thing to have in common.

Then we were too busy eating for questions. (Which isn't the worst problem to have. Especially when the food is your favorite.)

After dinner, we drank our sweet bean soup, which is a Chinese dessert, and all the adults gave me and Gwendolyn red envelopes (though she just tried to eat hers).

And even though everyone said, "She's too young, Cilla, she won't get it," when I was done eating, I gave Gwendolyn my chopsticks and tried to teach her how to use them.

Because these things are important.

And I wanted everyone in the restaurant to see that I could use chopsticks too, as well as my dad or Auntie Eva or Nai Nai or Ye Ye.

And that my sister would be just as good as I was, someday.

Plus, even though she didn't get them, Gwendolyn had a GREAT time banging the chopsticks on the table. And then I took them away and put them in my mouth and pretended they were walrus teeth, and Gwendolyn clapped. So I think it's a sign that she loves chopsticks and just needs to keep practicing.

We drove home full and tired and sticky. (That last part may have been my fault. I spilled some red bean soup on myself. And Gwendolyn. Also my mom.)

And even though I could see she was tired, Auntie Eva sat up with me while I got ready for bed, and she braided my hair while my dad read me a story.

That night I lay in bed and looked up at my mini-tent, and I started thinking about the year ahead. And I started worrying a little. Because even though I'd tried to leave enough oranges around for luck, I hadn't realized how MUCH luck I'll need, if I'm going to teach Gwendolyn how to use chopsticks, learn every Chinese wedding Tradition, AND meet Paul's Very Impressive, High-Powered family at Auntie Eva's wedding.

Though I guess I'm already doing all right, because it was very lucky to be chosen by Auntie Eva to be her flower girl. And when my mom didn't notice the orange under her pillow and woke up with sticky orange-juice hair, she thought it was so funny that she barely got mad.

Which is proof that this year is off to a *very* lucky start.

2

THIRD-GRADE RESOLUTIONS

Auntie Eva spent the whole weekend with us, and there was a lot of talk about weddings and families and flower girl details. All of this gave me a lot to think about (most of it VERY exciting).

But it wasn't until Monday, at school, that I realized it was time to write a new book.

When I got to school that morning, I couldn't wait to tell Colleen all about the wedding and Chinese New Year. In case you didn't read my last book and haven't met Colleen, she's my best friend. We met in kindergarten, when I was really shy, but she talked to me anyway. She's confident and tall and really good at sports, and she always knows what to say. Also, she's going to be an Olympic soccer player when she grows up, we've decided recently. Which is a GREAT destiny to have.

Colleen is the *best* best friend in the world, and she never lets me down. So when I told her about Auntie Eva's news, her reaction was everything I'd hoped it would be.

"I love weddings," Colleen said, clapping her hands. "Especially when they break the glass in front of everyone."

"Wow," I said. "I didn't know that happened."

"Did you say *weddings*, Silly?" Alien-Face McGee leaned toward us. He sits at our table, and he calls me "Silly" when he knows it's "Cill-*a*," and he likes to interrupt things. All of this makes him very annoying, and usually I tell him so. But I really wanted to talk about the wedding, so this was actually very convenient, even though my name is NOT "Silly."

"I like weddings. Especially trying to figure out the secret code for when to stand and when to kneel," he said.

(I made a note of this Tradition, plus the glass one, to ask about later.)

"Also, I was in a wedding," Alien-Face went on.

"Really?" Colleen asked.

"Yeah," he said. "I carried the rings, and my mom said that if I misbehaved I'd be grounded for the rest of my life, so it was pretty important that I got it right."

"Wow." I sighed. "And I thought being a flower girl was stressful."

Just then, Mr. Flight said, "Okay, everyone, time for Morning Announcements!" This is how we start every day. During Morning Announcements, Mr. Flight tells us the exciting things we'll be doing in class. He also takes attendance and tells us a new joke of the day. This is one of the (many) reasons Mr. Flight's third-grade class is amazing. (Even if Mr. Flight can't fly, and isn't even a pilot, which was disappointing to learn at the beginning of the school year.)

We also sometimes have sharing time in the

mornings, if someone's had a birthday or if there was a holiday or special occasion.

Which is why I was *especially* excited.

"So," Mr. Flight said. "This weekend was Chinese New Year. Did anyone here celebrate?"

"Me! Me!" I said, raising my hand. Melvin Liu also raised his hand, and we grinned at each other.

"Great!" Mr. Flight said. "Tell us about it."

"Well," I started, "Chinese New Year is really fun. It happens on a different day every year, and you go to Chinatown and there's a parade."

"Yeah," Melvin said. "And the date is always different because the Chinese calendar is a lunar calendar, which means it's based on the moon."

"Oh," I said. I hadn't known that. "Right. Also, there are lots of Traditions, like fireworks, and every shop puts oranges on chairs outside their doors for luck. And there are moon cakes and dumplings and giant fish."

"It's the best," Melvin said, nodding, and I smiled at him. "And you eat lots of the food because of their names. So in Chinese, fish are called '*yu*,' which also means 'prosperity,' so that's why you eat it."

"Oh," I said quietly. "Yeah." And I decided that I'd let him tell the rest.

After Morning Announcements, it was time for math. We all went to get a colored pencil from Mr. Flight's big box of supplies for our work sheets.

"Do you speak Chinese, Melvin?" Tim #2 asked, just behind me.

"Yeah." Melvin sighed. "I have to go to Chinese school *every* Sunday. It's REALLY boring."

"Huh," Tim #2 said. "But you don't, right, Cilla?" he asked.

"No," I admitted.

"Right, because you're not really Chinese," Tim said. "Just half. Oh, I want the red pencil!" he called out.

And then he was gone, leaving me standing there, blinking. And I didn't know what to do, or

how I felt, because no, I *am* Chinese. But then I remembered that the waiters in Chinatown hadn't thought so. And that Melvin knows so much more than I do about Chinese New Year and Traditions. And I wasn't sure what this all meant, and—

"Cilla!" Colleen came bouncing over to me. "I got the purple one for you and the teal for Melissa—your favorites!" So there was nothing to do but go back to my desk and learn about pie charts.

The rest of the morning was okay. I sit at a table with Colleen, Alien-Face McGee, and Melissa Hernandez, who's new to our school this year. In case you haven't read my last book, you should know that Alien-Face's real name is Ben McGee, but I call him "Alien-Face" because I made up a story about how he's really a (nice) alien in disguise who was sent to observe human beings.

Melissa's nice too, though she doesn't talk much and I'm not sure if she likes me. She does listen and smile a lot, though, especially during writing. We write A LOT in Mr. Flight's class, which is another reason that I love third grade. And we learn about things like Similes, which is when you compare one thing to something completely different, using the word "like" or "as" to describe it. So, for example, I might say, "Gwendolyn is as round as a caterpillar." Or, "My dad snores like an elephant." Or, "Someday, I will be as well-known as pizza."

Mr. Flight loves writing, though he's also big on something called Precision of Language. This means using the best words to say exactly what you mean. So, instead of saying, "Gwendolyn's diaper is the smelliest thing EVER," I could say, "Gwendolyn's diaper smells like a swamp," because it's more specific. Plus it's also a Simile.

Anyway, my point is that writing is great, and if we want to, we're allowed to share our work with our tables. And when I share my work, Melissa listens and smiles, and I think she thought the diaper Simile was really funny. But it's hard to tell because she never says anything, and then when I asked if I could see her Similes, she shook her head no, even though I think she let Colleen see them when I was sharing with Alien-Face McGee.

Which is strange.

After lunch, we had recess. We make up lots of excellent games at recess, and sometimes Mr. Flight comes out and does cartwheels on the grass. (So even if he can't fly, Mr. Flight does know some *excellent* tricks.)

Today, Alien-Face, the Tims, and Sally all ran over to the slide to play Dragon-Sorcerer-Warriors. Usually I love this game. It's part of a story I made up, and Colleen liked it so much that she wanted to be in it, and then Alien-Face and everyone else wanted to join. And people playing your stories is a BIG compliment.

But on Monday, I didn't feel like running over with them right away. Colleen stayed with me.

"Are you okay, Cilla?" she asked.

"Yeah." I nodded. "I was just thinking. . . . Do you think I should go to Chinese school?" I asked in a quiet voice. "It sounds fun."

"I dunno," she said. "Melvin says it's kind of boring."

"But he can speak Chinese. And I can't. That seems like something I should be able to do."

"Well . . ." She thought about this for a minute. "Maybe. But you can hold a headstand for three whole minutes, and he can't do that."

"Good point," I said. And then I smiled. "You're the best."

"Thanks." Colleen smiled back. "So are you."

"Also," I said, "I think I'll write a Classic. That's something Melvin won't do either. Or Tim #2, right?"

"Right." She grinned. "I can't wait to read it."

And we ran and joined the others to be dragon-sorcerer-warriors together.

FROGS IN THE KITCHEN
AND OTHER BAD IDEAS

Yesterday, I had an Adventure, which, as I've mentioned, is GREAT for Classics. Even better, my adventure has a moral, which is *very* Classic and means you learn something at the end of your story. And the moral of this story has to do with frogs. Because I wasn't the only one who had an Adventure this weekend. Harold, our third-grade classroom frog, had a BIG adventure too.

Harold lives in a tank above the science bookshelf in Mr. Flight's classroom. We take turns feeding him, and at the beginning of the year we got to learn all about him and how tadpoles turn into frogs. Every weekend, Harold gets to go home with a different student. He comes with an instruction sheet taped to his tank, and all you have to do is feed him and every once in a while change his water.

I think Harold is really fun. I want to train him to follow my finger when I trace it on the edges of his tank, and he used to float around close to it when I tried at the beginning of the year. But he's been kind of sleepy recently, and he doesn't seem to want to do any tricks. He does like to swim and float and kick his legs slowly, though. And when he taps at the floor of his tank, the water makes pretty swirls and bubbles. So I was excited when, on Friday, Mr. Flight reminded me that it was my turn to take Harold home for the weekend.

That day, Harold rode the bus with me and Colleen. We tried to get him to ribbit (he didn't) and only sloshed a little water onto the bus seat (I was very proud).

When I got off the bus, I ran to where my mom was waiting for me because I couldn't wait to introduce her to Harold.

But my mom maybe wasn't that excited to meet
him at first. In fact, she let out a little yell when she
saw me and said, "Young Lady, *what* is *that*?"

"Harold," I explained.

My dad, who had come to our front door bouncing Gwendolyn, put his hand to his mouth and tried not to laugh, but he did.

"Oookay," she said. "But where did he come from?"

"School," I said.

"No." She put her hand to her forehead. "I mean, why is he here?"

"Oh, because you signed the permission slip for us to take him home this weekend," I said. "At the beginning of the school year."

"Shouldn't Mr. Flight send home some reminders about, um, Harold?" my dad asked from the doorway.

"Oh, he did!" I said. "I forgot—they're all in my backpack. Wait, let me get them for you." I twisted around to open my bag, but it was hard with Harold's tank in my hands.

And then my mom laughed too.

"Well, I don't think we need them now," she said with a funny sigh. She reached down and took the tank from me. "Well, hello, Harold." She held the tank up so she could see Harold's face. But he just floated there.

As Harold does.

I think my mom and dad were worried that Harold would be a lot of work, but really he wasn't. And it was fun to show him around my house, and he liked meeting Gwendolyn because when she pointed to the tank and said, "Ga baba da!" he kicked his legs and made bubbles. So, when my mom told me that Gwendolyn and I would be spending Saturday with my Grandma and Grandpa Jenkins so she and my dad could visit an old friend, I really, really, REALLY wanted to take Harold along.

At first my mom said, "Absolutely not," which I didn't understand, because my Grandma and Grandpa love pets, not like Nai Nai and Ye Ye (who would never, ever, ever like Harold, because they don't like animals in the house). Plus Harold is MUCH nicer than Grandma and Grandpa Jenkins's new dog, whose name is Daisy and who is strange and sniffly and makes snorting noises wherever she goes.

But it looked like Harold would have to stay home alone, and I worried that he would be lonely and that maybe while we were gone a red-tailed hawk would break through the window and carry him away, because these things happen.

Luckily, when my Grandpa Jenkins came to pick us up, he saw Harold the moment he walked into the kitchen and said, "A frog! I love frogs! Where did he come from?"

So I came running over before my mom could answer and said, very fast, "His name is Harold and he's the classroom frog and he's super nice and he gets lonely by himself and can he please come to visit your house?" I gave Grandpa Jenkins my biggest smile.

"Of course!" Grandpa Jenkins said. "What fun. Why, I remember when I used to play with frogs behind my grandmother's house. We'd catch them in nets, you see. . . ."

My mom raised an eyebrow as she finished buttoning Gwendolyn's coat. "You're sure Mom will be okay with this?" she asked.

"Of course," my Grandpa Jenkins said, waving his hand like it was nothing. "She'll be delighted to meet Harold."

And my mom threw up her hands, which I know means "yes" and "sigh" all at once. So I jumped up and down and said, "Thank you, Grandpa!"

And that's how Harold, Gwendolyn, and I set

off on our Adventure. (Though of course, we didn't know it yet.)

It turned out that Grandma Jenkins wasn't as thrilled as Grandpa Jenkins had said she'd be. In fact, when she came outside wrapped in her bright green winter coat (which I LOVE) to help me and Gwendolyn (and Batman) out of the car, she said, "Oh. My," when she saw Harold in the tank. And then Grandpa Jenkins said, "It's just a frog, m'dear. I used to play with them all the time when I was younger."

Grandma Jenkins raised her eyebrows in a way that wasn't that convinced, and she looked just like my mom. But to be honest, I don't understand why Grandma Jenkins doesn't like Harold. Especially because, now, the moment you walk into her house, you meet—

"Daisy!" Grandpa Jenkins yelled, when we came in the door. "No jumping!"

But Daisy, who's a small black dog with a loopy tail and a squished-in face and big eyes like a bug's, didn't listen.

In fact, she never listens.

Daisy jumped up on my knees, snorting and drooling and wiggling her butt, and almost knocked me over, like she always does whenever I walk in.

I wouldn't necessarily mind this, because Colleen's dog, Spock, does it too. But I think Daisy's only interested in food, not like Spock, who wants you to scratch his ears or rub his belly. When you pet Daisy, all she does is jump around and try to nip your fingers, like she's checking if there's food there. And when you have food, you have to be REALLY careful because she'll leap up, and once she grabbed toast from my fingers and scratched them with her teeth.

So I don't really like Daisy.

And I think Harold is a MUCH better pet.

Grandma Jenkins put Harold's tank on a corner of the kitchen counter.

"Can I give him a tour of the house?" I asked.

"Um," Grandma said, "maybe later."

And then she went to go wash her hands.

I love spending days at Grandma and Grandpa Jenkins's house. We have lots of Traditions there. Grandma is excellent at math, and if I have any homework, she likes to help me. Sometimes we sit in her office, which is a room upstairs with big windows where she grades papers and keeps giant books on art. We do our work together, and she lets me take down the fancy certificate on the wall that says she's a "Dr. Jenkins," because the handwriting is beautiful and loopy and I like to trace it with my finger.

We have other Traditions there too, like how I go for a walk with Grandpa Jenkins when Gwendolyn is napping or how Grandma Jenkins and I bake cookies for dessert.

My Grandma Jenkins is also really big on being Proper, which is another kind of Tradition. It means she likes things like Table Manners, and candles on the dinner table, and forks and knives and spoons going in exactly the right place. And sometimes being Proper means poems that I've never heard before, like, "Cilla, Cilla, strong and able, get your elbows off the table."

So sometimes, being Proper isn't the most fun thing in the world. (Though I do like the candles at dinner.)

But it turns out that it was just what Harold needed.

It all started when I was sitting with Grandma Jenkins and Gwendolyn in the kitchen while Grandpa Jenkins was practicing the piano. He's just started piano lessons because he wants a new hobby. So far, he knows "Twinkle, Twinkle, Little Star" and can (almost) play "Mary Had a Little Lamb" with no (big) mistakes. We usually go into the kitchen when he plays because there are only so many times you can hear these two songs, though

Daisy stays out with him and sometimes barks along. Which is funny.

Grandma was just getting a glass of water when she started looking in the tank with a little frown.

"That water doesn't look clean," she said.

"Huh." I went over to look too. "Mr. Flight asked Billy if he cleaned it last weekend, and he said yes. Though I guess it's always kind of cloudy . . . Oh!" I said suddenly. "We can ask Grandpa Jenkins when he's done playing—he says he's a frog expert!"

"Why, what an excellent idea, Cilla," Grandma Jenkins said. "I'll tell you what. When your grandfather's done, I'll ask him to clean the tank. We'll give Harold some new, nicely filtered water. I think that should cheer him up."

"Wow, Grandma," I said, giving her a hug. "That's really nice of you! Will Grandpa Jenkins mind?"

"Not at all." She patted my back. "It was your grandfather's idea to bring Harold over. And a good host looks after his guest. It's the Proper thing to do."

And she smiled and I smiled back, because who knew that being Proper could be so GREAT?

Grandpa Jenkins said, "What?" when he heard our plan, and then, "Um, sure," when he saw Grandma Jenkins's expression. And we found an old goldfish bowl in the basement and cleaned it so Harold could stay there while we refilled his tank. Grandpa Jenkins couldn't quite touch him without jumping, so I had to move Harold back and forth. Then we washed out the tank, and Grandpa said, "Yuck," because Grandma was right, it WAS dirty, and it smelled not that great, and my hands felt slimy with algae. And then we put in clean, filtered water from a bottle and put all of Harold's rocks and plants back in, and finally, Harold went back in too.

I watched to see if he'd have a reaction, and I thought maybe he'd ribbit or do a backflip or wave to say thank you, but he didn't do anything.

He just sat, floating and blinking in the water, like usual.

"Don't forget to clip the tank shut," Grandma Jenkins said.

And I was going to.

But Harold still looked kind of sad, so I put the lid on but didn't quite clip it, because I wanted him to get extra air.

"Well," Grandpa Jenkins said from the sink, where he was washing his hands *again*, "we've done our duty, Cilla dear. Now I think I'll go shower. That smell . . ."

He shook his head and walked out of the kitchen, and Grandma, who was sitting at the table bouncing Gwendolyn, winked at me, and I winked back.

Grandma had shut Daisy out of the kitchen while we cleaned Harold's tank, and as soon as Grandpa left the door open behind him she ran in, straight into a little bit of spilled algae water. Then she jumped up to see if I had any food (which

I didn't). But she loved the algae smell and started rolling around in the puddle before I realized what she was doing. Which meant Grandma Jenkins had to give her a bath in the kitchen sink. I helped, and Daisy did NOT like it. She yelped and snorted the whole time, and when she got out she raced around and jumped up on ME, and then I smelled like algae plus dog shampoo, and I said, "No, Daisy! I don't have any food for you—get down!"

So Grandma Jenkins made me take a bath (which was a BIG Theme that day, as you can tell), and I put on a pair of pajamas that I keep at her house, because everything else had a wet-dog-frog smell.

After I was clean, I sat on the floor with Gwendolyn and played with her while Grandma Jenkins started cooking and Grandpa Jenkins watched the news. Grandma Jenkins came to join us when she was done, and we all sat together (another nice Tradition at their house). Grandpa Jenkins did his embroidery, and Grandma Jenkins held Daisy in her lap and brushed her so Gwendolyn could stay on the floor and we didn't have to worry about Daisy chewing her toys.

We were all talking, and playing, and brushing, and embroidering, when all of a sudden, we heard a bang in the kitchen.

"What was that?" I asked, looking up.

"Did something fall?" Grandpa Jenkins asked, turning around.

Then we heard a sound.

A deep sound. A loud sound. Like a song.

But instead of words, it was saying, "Riiiib-biiiiiiiiit."

"Oh my!" Grandma Jenkins said.

We jumped up and ran to the kitchen, where my Grandma's pot roast was sitting out cooling. A jar of olives had been knocked over right next to it.

Next to that was the tank, with the lid knocked to the side.

And below it all, in the middle of the kitchen

floor, was a puffed-out, wide-eyed, VERY happy frog.

"Grandma, you're a genius!" I threw out my hands. "He's so much better!"

"OH MY GOODNESS GRACIOUS!" Grandma Jenkins said.

"Golly!" Grandpa Jenkins said.

"Riiiiibbit," Harold said, puffing out his chest.

"Bababoo!" Gwendolyn said. She waved Batman around in the air and seemed very happy to see Harold.

And just then, "Ararararararararah!" Daisy came running into the kitchen, barking.

"Oh no!" I shouted.

"Daisy!" Grandpa Jenkins grabbed for her. He missed.

"RIBBIT," Harold said. He looked Daisy right in the eyes, he made one giant hop toward her, and—

"SCREECH!" Daisy screamed and leaped

backward as Harold landed with a "plop" right in front of her. She ran and hid behind Grandma Jenkins. Who was hiding behind me.

"Bagaboo!" Gwendolyn clapped from Grandma Jenkins's arms, because to be fair, it WAS pretty great.

And Harold was very brave. Which is what Adventures are all about.

"Come on, Harold," I said, slowly walking toward him. "Come on. . . ." I jumped and grabbed him.

"Get the tank!" my Grandma yelled.

And Grandpa Jenkins went to get it, and I ran to plop Harold in, but suddenly Harold pushed against my hand and I didn't realize how strong he was, and he leaped right toward the counter where Grandma Jenkins had left a knife in the center and . . .

We gasped as Harold missed it by an inch. I raced toward him, and Grandpa did too, but he leaped again, toward—

"The disposal!" Grandpa Jenkins yelled.

"NO, HAROLD!" I yelled.

"Cover the drain!" Grandpa yelled.

"And the pot roast!" Grandma yelled.

We all moved at once. I grabbed a small bowl sitting on the edge of the counter and . . . caught him JUST in time, as he leaped toward the drain.

"Oh." Grandma Jenkins sighed. "My gravy . . ."

"Oops," I said, looking in bowl, where Harold blinked at me through a sticky brown mess. "Sorry, Grandma." And then, "Sorry, Harold," as I carefully rinsed him off.

Because, as I had already learned with Daisy that day, pets DO NOT like baths.

I put Harold safely back in the tank, and Grandma said, "How did that happen? Was the tank lid shut?"

Then I said "Oops" again, and my face got red. Grandma Jenkins shook her head but also laughed, and we made sure it was latched this time (though, of course, we left the vents open so he could get air). And the best part is, Harold seemed really happy to be home. He sat in his tank, puffing out his throat and ribbiting. And Daisy clearly liked it because she began to howl.

"Well," my Grandma Jenkins said, as she rinsed out the gravy bowl. "What a to-do!"

"Yes," I said. "There was A LOT to do, wasn't there?"

"Indeed." She put her hands on her hips, which is always how you know she means business. "Well, have you learned anything from this, Young Lady?"

And this is where the moral comes in, because she was right, I HAD learned something.

"Yes," I said. "The next time I bring Harold home, I'll only let him in the bathroom or the living room. The kitchen's waaaay too dangerous."

On Monday, my mom drove me to school so I could take Harold in safely. She told Mr. Flight about Harold's adventures, and Mr. Flight said, in this order: "Wow, Harold!" And then, "Good job, Cilla." And then, "Sorry about that, Ellen. Please thank your parents for me."

Then he made up a new instruction sheet, with a cleaning schedule and a reminder in bright purple letters that frogs need filtered water to keep them healthy.

And as if all this wasn't enough, there was one more surprise that day.

Because when Harold the frog, who had never made a sound in class before, began singing, very loudly and happily in the middle of a silent math quiz, Mr. Flight jumped REALLY high, and said, "Oh my goodness gracious!" and sounded *just* like Grandma Jenkins.

Which was another GREAT moral to learn.

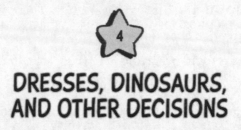

DRESSES, DINOSAURS, AND OTHER DECISIONS

My Grandma says that time flies when you're having fun.

This used to confuse me, because wouldn't time need wings, and I have A LOT of fun and I've never seen anything except birds and airplanes fly.

But I'm learning now that words don't always mean exactly what they say.

This is good to know, actually, because I got REALLY worried when my dad said that after Auntie Eva's wedding, we'd tear up the dance floor. Because I'm sure Auntie Eva paid a lot of money for that floor, and aren't weddings supposed to be nice, and you're not supposed to break things, and WHY WOULD YOU DO SUCH A THING?!

But then my dad reminded me about expressions.

And explained that this was an expression that meant we'd have fun dancing.

Which was a BIG relief.

Anyway, my point is that now I understand what Grandma Jenkins was saying a bit more, about time flying (even if it doesn't have wings), because she just means that when you're having fun, time goes by quickly. And this is very true. Because school's been really, really fun, and I've been going over to Colleen's house a lot, and playing with Gwendolyn, and spending time with my family. And now all this time has passed, and I haven't done any writing in a few weeks, and it didn't seem like long at all.

And I might not even have noticed that lots of time was passing, except for the fact that yesterday, Colleen told me that soccer season was starting soon.

At first, I didn't think a lot about it.

Until today at recess, when it came up again in a *big* way.

It all started with a dinosaur game that I'd made up earlier this week. I'd come up with some new ideas for it and thought maybe we could be fire-breathing dinosaurs at recess. So I was excited to tell Colleen my plan.

Except that when I ran out to the playground, I turned around and Colleen wasn't there.

She was still standing by the lunchroom door, talking with Melissa Hernandez, Sasha Simpson, and a few other kids from the soccer team.

I walked over to them, and I was sure that Colleen would say goodbye or invite them to join our game, because we spend *every* recess together.

So I didn't know what to say, or what to do, when Colleen came over to me with a funny kind of look on her face.

"Cilla, Melissa was just telling me that some of the kids from soccer want to play kickball today. And, um, I think I'm going to play with them."

"Oh," I said, in a small voice.

"You could play too," Colleen said, twisting her hands.

But we both knew that wouldn't happen. Because I don't like kickball. And Colleen knows it, just like she knows everything else about me.

"No," I said, quietly. "But . . . thank you."

Suddenly it seemed like neither of us knew what to say, and Colleen ALWAYS knows what to say, plus we're best friends, so we shouldn't have moments like this. It's a rule.

I didn't know what to do.

"Hey!" Alien-Face McGee came skipping over. "Sally told me you're going to play kickball, Colleen. Want to be their cheerleaders, Cilla? We can pretend to make pyramids, and maybe our pom-poms can shoot fire."

"Yeah," I said, slowly.

"Yeah!" Colleen said at the same time.

Soon the funny feeling went away. I was excited to watch Colleen and to cheer for her, and maybe to convince Alien-Face to be fire-breathing dinosaur cheerleaders, which would be extra exciting.

But I also hoped that kickball wouldn't be an everyday thing.

Colleen is a great player, and Melissa is too. And they high-fived whenever they passed each other and seemed to have lots of sports jokes.

But, to be fair, Alien-Face and I also had a lot of jokes, and sometimes we were giggling or roaring so much that we couldn't really cheer, but I think it's the thought that counts.

And then when we got bored in the second half of the game, Alien-Face showed me some new monkey-bar tricks.

Tim #2 came to play with us toward the end of recess and started telling us about the fun things he was doing after school that day. I was excited

too, because it was my day with Nai Nai, and we were going to Chinatown, and I opened my mouth to tell him and Alien-Face all about it.

But I realized I maybe didn't want to.

So I just said my grandma and I were going to spend time together.

And Tim #2 said, "Neat!" Which was nice of him.

After school, Nai Nai picked me up, and we went to Chinatown together, which we do every week. Usually we laugh and talk and make jokes the whole time. But today, she was kind of quiet. And maybe even a little upset.

"Are you okay, Nai Nai?" I asked, when we'd gotten out of the car.

She patted my hand.

"Yes," she said. "It's just been a long day. With some wedding things."

"Oh," I said.

"Nothing for you to worry," she said.

"Okay," I said.

And then she smiled, but it wasn't her normal Nai Nai smile.

So I decided to tell funny stories to make her feel better.

I told her all about Mr. Flight, and my games with Colleen, and then Harold, because that was a story all about cheering up and making someone happy. (Though I didn't tell her about kickball, because as I've mentioned, that's a one-time thing.)

I think Nai Nai enjoyed my stories, even if she did say "Ay yah!" and "In the house?!" when I told her about Harold. And when I said maybe she could meet Harold someday and promised her that she'd like him, she said, "Hmmmm."

Which is Nai Nai's way of saying "No" or "I'm not convinced" or "Absolutely not, Young Lady."

But nicely.

My stories made her laugh, though, and she mussed my hair and didn't seem to be feeling quiet anymore. So I think they helped.

Afterward, just before we went home, Nai Nai

took me to her favorite bakery to get min bauu, which are Chinese bread rolls that Ye Ye and I LOVE.

The shop was busy and full of the warm smell of bread, sweet rolls, and custard.

I held Nai Nai's hand and listened to the people talking and laughing all around us. It was a nice, familiar sound.

A sound I've always loved.

But suddenly, I thought about school, and Melvin, and Tim #2. And I realized how much of the sounds around me I didn't understand.

"Nai Nai," I asked, "will you teach me Chinese?"

Nai Nai smiled a big smile. A *real* smile.

"Of course," she said.

"So I can speak it before the wedding?" I asked.

"Wah," she said. "I don't think so."

"Oh." I tried not to let her see that I was disappointed. But Nai Nai took my hand and gave it a squeeze and said, "Tell me what you want to say. I can teach you small things before the wedding."

"Oh!" I said. "Okay." And I squeezed her hand back.

"Why before the wedding?" she asked.

"It's a surprise," I said.

"Wah," she said. "I love surprises."

"Me too," I said with a smile. Then it was our turn to order, and Nai Nai got me a box of almond cookies to take home, which was an *excellent* surprise (so I'm glad she likes them).

When I got home, my mom explained that Nai Nai had been upset because that morning, Auntie Eva had asked her to wear a different dress to the wedding, even though she'd already bought a lacy blue one. Apparently, Paul's mom is something called a Stickler for Tradition, so Auntie Eva felt like she couldn't argue.

"This is normal wedding Drama, sweetie," my mom said when she saw my worried expression. "Bringing together two families always means making choices like this, and sometimes those choices upset people. But Nai Nai understands. To be honest, I don't think Nai Nai really minds about the dress. She just wants to be a part of Auntie Eva's Big Day. And Paul's parents live closer than she does, so I think she's worried that they'll be really involved in the wedding, and she won't."

"Oh," I said. "Do you think that will happen?"

"Not at all," my mom said. "It's really nothing to worry about."

"Hmmmm," I said.

Just then Gwendolyn started Fussing. So I never got to ask what the Traditions that Paul's mom cared so much about were. And I wish I knew, because now there's even *more* that I don't know about weddings and Traditions and Chinese Customs.

So, I've decided that I need to start flower girl practice NOW. Because I've always known that Nai Nai and Auntie Eva sometimes don't Get Along when she visits, which is why Auntie Eva stays at our house instead of with Nai Nai and Ye Ye.

But I didn't know that they also didn't Get Along when it came to weddings, which are supposed to be happy.

And I want Auntie Eva to enjoy her wedding, and I want her to see that it's really a GREAT idea to have our family involved in her Big Day.

Plus, if everything goes perfectly, and if I'm the best flower girl EVER, I bet Auntie Eva and Nai Nai will forget that they ever had hurt feelings.

Now my dad's Skyping with Auntie Eva to make sure she isn't upset, because he says that's what big brothers do. I got to stay up late to say hello to her just before I went to bed. She told me all about how she'd found the most beautiful dress for me and said she'd send a picture so I could see it. She sounded happy, so it seemed like the Not Getting Along had passed.

Which was a relief.

But before I left the room, I heard another part

of their conversation, after I'd said good night to her. I was supposed to be brushing my teeth, but I'd gotten distracted by some colorful erasers my dad had brought home from work. So I was still there when I heard Auntie Eva say, "I don't know what I'd do without you, big brother. I had no idea that there'd be so many choices to make between people. And I've always gotten along with Paul's parents, so I thought that blending the two families would be easy. I hope they like each other.

"But," she went on, "at least everyone seems fine. And I think I've figured out the maid of honor too. At the end of the day, Jane is really my best friend now. I still feel kind of guilty, though. Karen was my best friend in college, and she was there for me during some tough times. But we've just grown apart, you know? And . . . I don't know. It's hard to choose between best friends."

"She'll understand, sis," my dad said. "Maybe you can have Karen read a poem or do something else in the ceremony. . . ." And then he started saying more, but I didn't hear, because right around then my mom came in and said, "Excuse me, Young Lady, but does this look like teeth brushing?"

So I had to go.

Because when your parents call you Young Lady, it means it's time to get serious.

Now I'm in bed, writing, because this conversation, and this day, has given me a lot to think about.

Like how even though Drama is exciting and good in books, I'd rather not have it in my family.

Besides, Blending two families sounds like a VERY hard thing, and I should know because it took a long time for my families to Blend.

For a long time, I worried that it would never happen.

And now, I wonder what will happen if Paul's family doesn't like Nai Nai, or Ye Ye, or my dad, or even me. And even worse, what if Auntie Eva decides she likes Paul's family more than ours? Because there are fewer disagreements and everyone Gets Along?

And most of all, I can't stop thinking about what Auntie Eva said.

Because how could someone ever choose between something like two moms or two best friends?

And what happens if you're not the one they pick?

CHANGE IS STRANGE (EXCEPT WHEN THERE'S PIZZA INVOLVED)

My mom says I need to be something called "better with change." I don't think she's quite right, because I'm GREAT with change—like how I agreed to move my Selena Moon paper dolls from the bottom shelf in my bookcase to the top so Gwendolyn couldn't get them. That was a BIG change, and I was *completely* fine with it.

But I do know that sometimes, changes make me nervous. Like how worried I was before Gwendolyn came, which seems funny now because I really like her and one of my favorite parts of the day is when I come home from school and play with her and boop her nose and help her build (or destroy, depending on how she's feeling) block towers.

So I'm learning that change can be okay, even if you're not sure about it. But I'd prefer if it didn't happen too much.

Especially all at once, like it did today.

While I was getting ready for school this morning, I thought more about what Auntie Eva had said, and I decided I'd ask Colleen to pinky-swear-promise to always be best friends with each other and no one else.

So we'd never have any Drama about who was the best friend of all.

The timing was perfect too, because I was going to Colleen's house after school. Colleen and I have Traditions of our own at her house, and we play games and make up stories and have the most fun EVER (as best friends should). So I knew it would be easy to have the pinky-swear-promise talk there.

But right before lunch, Mr. Usmani from the office came in with a note for Mr. Flight, and he took Colleen and Melissa aside.

And at lunch, Colleen told me what the note had said.

Melissa's mom had to stay at work late, and she'd asked Colleen's mom if Melissa could come over after school.

"I'm sorry it won't be just us," Colleen said. "But Melissa's actually really nice. Our moms are friends, so she's come over a few times before. I think you'll like playing with her."

"Oooooookay," I said. But I wasn't so sure.

Melissa rode our bus home, which meant that Colleen and I couldn't play our normal bus games. And when we got to Colleen's house, Colleen's dad had THREE half-sandwiches made and said, "Melissa! Peanut butter and banana—just the way you like it!" And I'd known that Melissa had been over to Colleen's house before, but I hadn't realized that it was so many times that her dad knows the snacks she likes.

Then Melissa kept saying things like "We should play with your kazoos, Colleen" and "Has Cilla seen your new puzzle?" But she didn't say much to me at all. And sometimes, she'd go over to Colleen and *whisper*, and then Colleen would say, "Hey, why don't we play with my chemistry set. . . ."

Even worse, Melissa knew our couch-to-couch jumping game and how to rub Spock's ear in the way that makes his leg go up and down. Which are special things that Colleen and I do together.

Melissa's mom came to pick her up just a few minutes before mine did.

"So, does Melissa come over a lot?" I asked, as her car drove away.

"Kind of," Colleen said. "But mostly because her mom and my mom are friends, and they talk while we do our homework," she added quickly.

Which I know she said to make me feel better.

But I didn't.

I thought about how Melissa whispers to Colleen all the time. And how she doesn't talk to me. And how she's the one who's been putting together kickball games at recess and making Colleen choose between them and me.

Suddenly, I understood.

Melissa Hernandez is plotting to make Colleen *her* best friend, instead of mine.

And that's a change I won't let happen.

My mom picked me up, and I was happy to be going home to do all the things I always do after school, like play with Gwendolyn and help my dad cook dinner because I'm his Official Helper. I knew things at home, at least, would be normal. And then I'd have time to think about Melissa's Evil Plot. And how to foil it. (Which are two VERY Classic Themes, so at least this development is literary even if it's not great.)

But when I walked into the house, my dad ran to the door holding Gwendolyn.

"Ellen, Cilla," he said in an excited voice, "Gwendolyn said her first word! We were sitting on the rug, just a minute ago, and she said, 'Dada'!"

"What!" My mom and I rushed over.

"Dada!" Gwendolyn said, giggling and throwing her arms out like it was a fun game.

"Yay!" we all cheered.

"Her first word!" my mom said in a high, funny kind of voice.

Then there was a lot of running around and getting a camera and taking a video for my grandparents, and we all went to sit on the living room rug, where we keep Gwendolyn's toys.

"Now say 'Mama,'" my mom said. And Gwendolyn laughed and tried to chew my mom's fingers. But then she said "Ma," and we all clapped and my mom hugged her.

"My turn!" I said. "Now say 'Cilla'!" I said, bouncing up and down. "Come on, Gwendolyn, you can do it! Cilla."

"Dada ma baba da," Gwendolyn said, happily.

"No, Gwendolyn." I tried again. "SILL-LA." And I spoke very slowly, just like my mom had done, so I figured she'd get it.

"Dada ba rara!" she gurgled.

"Sweetheart," my mom said. "It's going to be a while before she can say something like 'Cilla.' Sounds like the ones in 'Mama' and 'Dada' are easier for babies, but 's' sounds and 'l' sounds are hard. You're going to have to be patient with her."

"Hmmm," I said.

Because this didn't seem all that fair.

Plus if she wasn't going to say anything else, the excitement should be over.

And we needed to be getting ready for dinner, and tonight was spaghetti night, and I get to help sprinkle the cheese and make the garlic bread. It's a Tradition.

My dad's phone rang, and it was Nai Nai, who was excited because she'd gotten the video he'd sent. And then my mom's phone rang too, and it was Grandpa Jenkins. And suddenly, my mom was saying, "Why don't we invite them all over for dinner, Nathan? We can get pizza."

"Great idea!" he said, taking out his phone again.

"Yay!" I said. (Because pizza is always a good change.)

"Though, tell your parents not to bring Daisy," my dad said. "My parents won't like her."

"They really don't like pets, do they?" I asked. "Why is that?"

"It's just how they've always been," he said with a shrug.

"Ah," I said. "A Tradition."

"Sure." He laughed as he dialed. "It's a kind of Tradition." And then Nai Nai picked up the phone, and he started talking in Chinese.

I was glad I'd learned another Tradition and made sure to write it down later—Chinese people don't like dogs.

This was nice to know, because I also don't like Daisy, so I'm just like my Nai Nai and Ye Ye.

Though I do like Spock, but I think that's an okay exception because Spock is the best.

And Harold, but he's a classroom frog, not a pet, so that doesn't count.

* * *

My Nai Nai and Ye Ye came over with red bean cupcakes and said "Wah!" when Gwendolyn said "Dada" and then "Mama."

And Grandma and Grandpa Jenkins brought a chocolate cake, and Grandma Jenkins said, "What an advanced baby! You know, you weren't even talking at this age, Cilla."

Which also made me say, "Hmmmmm."

But at least I got to go to the store with my dad to pick up the pizza, which is like being his Kitchen Helper (also: pizza). Plus there was LOTS of cake, and you know my feelings about that.

At dinner, Grandma and Grandpa Jenkins asked about the wedding, and Nai Nai seemed MUCH happier and didn't even mention the dress. She told Grandma and Grandpa Jenkins that they'd be getting their invitations any day now, because in Chinese weddings, you invite all the extended family (which was news to me, but good news). This made my Grandma Jenkins REALLY happy too, and she gave Nai Nai a hug.

And even though I was still upset about Melissa and the whole not-saying-Cilla thing, I remembered that some changes can be nice.

Because we'd never had dinner together like this, as a family, before my last book. In fact, my grandparents never really saw each other at all. And now, we do things together as a family, like have dinner sometimes and, apparently, go to Big Events together.

And it's really nice to see my grandmas get along.

Even if they will never agree on things like Daisy.

And even if they *did* spend pretty much all dinner talking about Gwendolyn.

* * *

When everyone left, I helped my dad dry the dishes while my mom put Gwendolyn in her pajamas.

"Do you think Gwendolyn will be a writer when she grows up?" I asked suddenly.

"Um, I don't know, sweetheart," my dad said with a little laugh. "Probably not."

"But she's Advanced," I said. "So she could be, if she wanted to."

My dad put a soapy arm around me.

"Sure," he said. "She can be anything she wants to be, and so can you. But I'm guessing she'll have a lot of interests of her own. I really wouldn't worry about it."

"Hmmmm," I said again.

Drying dishes gave me time to make a plan, though. And when I went to keep Gwendolyn company on the rug, where she was chewing on Batman, so my mom could help my dad finish the cleaning before bedtime, I realized I knew *exactly* what to do.

At school, I just have to show Colleen that I'm the greatest friend ever and much more fun to be around than Melissa. So all I have to do is to be a perfect best friend. And she'll forget all about Melissa and kickball.

And as for Gwendolyn . . .

I sat down next to her, put Batman to the side, and picked her up so she could look into my eyes, because this was Very Serious.

"Gwendolyn," I asked, "what are you?"

"Brrr-pa," she gurgled.

"No, focus, Gwendolyn," I said. "You can be anything you want to be, isn't that exciting? Anything except a writer. Do you understand, Gwen?" I said. "No writing. Also, 'Cilla'! Say it with me now! Also, 'chopsticks'! Can you say that? This is all very important."

But Gwendolyn just laughed and squirmed because she wanted to chew on her toes. And it didn't really seem like I was winning on this particular day. So I gave up and lay on the floor next to her and pretended I was eating my toes too, and she giggled. And then, very suddenly, she rolled over, curled up against my side, and put her head on my shoulder.

Which I think means she appreciates all the work I'm doing for her.

Which was a nice kind of change.

6

SPRING BREAK REFLECTIONS

My mom always tells me to slow down.

She says I can get carried away, and that I do something called jumping to conclusions and over-reacting and not paying attention.

But I know that none of this is true.

Because I pay attention to LOTS of things, like I notice whenever Colleen wears her favorite blue skirt with galaxies on it (if she can't be an Olympic soccer player, her backup plan is an astronaut). Or, more recently, whenever Melissa Hernandez does something else in her Evil Plot to take Colleen. Like when she whispers something to Colleen in class, and Colleen laughs. Or when I ask Colleen if

Melissa's been to her house again, and that funny look comes over Colleen's face, and it feels like she doesn't want to talk and we don't know what to say. Which I think means that Melissa's Evil Plot is working and Colleen is keeping things from me and doesn't want me to know that Melissa's winning her over.

This isn't jumping to a conclusion—it's being observant and seeing the whole story and filling in the rest.

Which are all skills that every good writer needs.

Right now, we're on spring break. Colleen's away visiting her grandma and grandpa, which is sad because she's not here but nice because I get a break from worrying that she and Melissa are having playdates without me.

So far, I've been doing A LOT in my plan to be the *best* best friend ever. I've been laughing extra loudly at Colleen's jokes and I always have a new story to tell her when I get on the bus. I even asked Alien-Face McGee about Melissa at recess on the day before break, when Melissa and Colleen were playing kickball (again!). But that was a bit strange, and I don't think he understood what was going on. Because when I asked, "What do you think of Melissa?" he said, "I dunno." He was hanging off the edge of the slide, kicking the ground with his feet. "She's nice."

"Sure," I said. "But are her stories good? Is she funny? How many shadow puppets can she make with just her hands? Is she real best friend material?"

"Um," he said. "I don't know. Do you want me to go and ask her?"

"No." I sighed.

"Why are you asking all these questions?" he asked.

"No reason." I sighed again, Dramatically, because Drama is always useful in a story (even when it's not all that fun).

"Are you looking for another best friend?"

"NO," I said, crossing my arms. "I'm happy with just ONE. I don't need any other best friends. Colleen is good enough for me, and all I want to do at recess is play with *her*."

"Oh," he said. And the way he said it made me look at him funny, because he sounded kind of sad.

I didn't feel any better about Colleen and Melissa. And I didn't think Alien-Face had understood the situation. Or what Melissa is trying to do. And I don't get why he Changed the Subject quickly after that, or why he went to go play with Tim #1 a few minutes later.

But Alien-Face seemed fine after recess. We waved goodbye before leaving for break, and he even promised he'd bring me back a pinecone from his camping trip.

My family also went on a trip, right at the start of the break. We went to visit Auntie Eva at her house, because it's her birthday soon.

The ride down took a looooong time, but it was fun. I kept waiting for unexpected moments and then saying "Gwendolyn, what are you!?" Because Destiny works in funny ways. But she'd just giggle, which isn't helpful. But I did learn other things about Gwendolyn, like how "The Wheels on the Bus" is her favorite song. She wanted someone to sing it to her over and over, and every time the singing stopped, she'd start to Fuss. And she'd say, "Buh! Buh!" (which is almost a word, and also *not* "Cilla"). Then my mom would say, "I can't stand it, not again." But then Gwendolyn would start to cry, and my dad would sigh and say, "Ellen." So my mom would make a huffing sound and say *"Fine,"* and then one of us would sing again.

Auntie Eva lives in a big, beautiful house. It's made of brick, and it's attached to a row of other brick houses. But Auntie Eva's house is the prettiest one. Her front porch has glass windows, and she's hung little twinkling lights all around them, and there's a big rocking chair with lots of pillows for sitting and reading and looking outside.

I was disappointed, but also relieved, when I found out that Paul would be traveling the weekend we were there, so we wouldn't meet him. Because that meant I'd have Auntie Eva all to myself, just like it's always been.

When we drove up, Auntie Eva was standing on the porch waving, like she always does. We brought our things in and took off our shoes and ordered takeout for dinner (which is always a very special treat). Afterward, she showed me the new triceratops puzzle she'd ordered just for me, and I started putting it together on the living room floor while my dad bounced Gwendolyn and he and my mom and Auntie Eva talked on the couch.

It was a great puzzle. So I stopped paying attention to their conversation because I really wanted to make the triceratops's face. And every once in a while, I'd hear Auntie Eva say things like "Yeah, it was a rough week at work. But it's okay—I'm just tired" and "Oh, man, Paul's dad *really* wants to have two kinds of cake, but I just don't care" and

"Mom wants me to go around and take pictures at every single table for *each* outfit change. Do you know how long that would take?"

Until right as I was about to put together the triceratops's tail, I heard a conversation that made me stop and pay attention.

They were still talking about the wedding. And my mom said, "Just remember, this is your day. All that matters is you and Paul. Everyone else will deal."

"Yeah," my dad said. "Also, the trick is knowing how to manage Mom. She can be a handful, but you just have to know how to keep her happy."

"That's easy for you to say, big brother," Auntie Eva said. "You're the son—you just have to show up and be yourself and you'll make Mom and Dad happy. I have to be *perfect*. And anytime I do something differently, Mom panics. Remember how she didn't want me buying this house, because that would somehow make me less likely to find a husband?"

"Yeah." My mom sighed. "I didn't quite get the logic there. I would've said yes to you so much sooner if you'd had a house like this," she said to my dad with a joking look.

"Good to know," he said with a laugh. But then he said, more seriously, "You're right, sis. I know you have it a lot harder. The old Traditions are hard to shake, I guess. They do it out of love, you know?"

"I do." Auntie Eva put a hand on my dad's. "And, hey, once this wedding's over, what else will they have to bug me about?"

"Kids," my mom and dad said at the same time.

Just then Gwendolyn started to Fuss, and my mom said, "Right on cue," and my dad said, "I think it's time for bed, Cilla."

So I didn't hear any more.

And I wanted to know what kinds of Traditions they were talking about and what they had to do with Auntie Eva's house.

But my dad put Gwendolyn down for a second, and she crawled toward the puzzle pieces, and then I was distracted trying to pull the triceratops's foot out of her mouth.

So I didn't ask.

Auntie Eva had lots of fun things planned for our trip. The next day we had breakfast at her favorite diner, and we squished into soft red booths and ate waffles. Then we went to a museum, where there were dinosaur skeletons and an exhibit on stars and planets. Auntie Eva and I took pictures next to the bones of a T. rex, and we pretended we were T. rexes too. And a few adults walked by us and gave Auntie Eva funny looks because we were both stomping around and making T. rex noises. But Auntie Eva didn't care.

We took a lot of silly photos that day, and my dad LOVED the galaxy exhibit. And in the gift shop, my mom said I could get some (very small) presents for my friends, so I got a small globe with the galaxy inside for Colleen. And, after a moment, I decided to get another small globe—this one with a dinosaur inside—for Alien-Face. Because I thought he'd really like it.

When we got home, Auntie Eva and Gwendolyn and my dad all went to take a nap, because my dad says that's what vacations are for. My mom and I sat on the couch to read our books. Gwendolyn

didn't nap for
very long (she never
does), and my dad
brought her down soon,
followed by Auntie Eva, who
still looked very sleepy and who had a GIANT
fluffy white bathrobe wrapped around her over her
clothes.

"Wow," my dad said, raising his eyebrows. "Good look."

"I get cold easily." Auntie Eva sniffed, and she frowned, but the corners of her mouth were turning up and her voice sounded like she was trying not to smile.

"Plus it'll make a great snow monster costume, if you ever need one," I pointed out.

"Yes! See?" she said to my dad. "I'm all set for Halloween."

"Oooh, and you could sew red eyes onto a white hat and put fake claws on white gloves, and you could wave your hands around when you roared, and it would be EXTRA scary!" I said, holding my arms out like a snow monster.

"Amazing!" Auntie Eva said, holding her arms out like a snow monster too.

"The family resemblance is uncanny," my dad said, shaking his head.

But Auntie Eva and I were too busy making snow monster sounds to respond. And my dad laughed at us, and it was a fun game.

My mom and dad wanted to make Auntie Eva a special birthday dinner that night, so my mom began getting Gwendolyn's coat on for a grocery store run.

"Nathan and I will both go, so we can be quick," my mom said, "and I don't want to leave this one in your hair."

"Do I have to go?" I asked.

"Cilla's welcome to stay with me," Auntie Eva

said, trying not to yawn. "I'm still waking up, so I don't know how much fun I'll be." She gave me a sleepy smile. "But we can hang out and have hot chocolate."

So then I had to jump up and down and be a happy snow monster, which was another excellent game.

Auntie Eva and I sat on the couch, drinking our hot chocolate. She was very quiet, though. For a minute, I worried I was being boring.

But then she leaned her head back on the couch pillow and let out a small, happy sigh.

"This is so nice, Cilla," she said, turning to me with a smile. "I never get to just sit in the quiet. When I'm by myself I'm always working or running around with this wedding. And then when I'm with the rest of the family, I'm always on, or worried about what they're thinking or what they need. I love that we can just sit together."

"Yeah." I smiled back. "It is nice."

Auntie Eva sank back even more into the couch cushions.

"Yeah," she said. "You know, it's so easy to get caught up in things, when you're a grown-up. I just have to take a deep breath and step back from it all. Like all this wedding stuff. I know my mom is just trying to take care of me. And it's always been hard for her, that I'm not as Traditional as she is. We fought a lot when I was younger. I wanted to be what I thought was 'normal'—to be American, not Chinese. And I've changed a lot since then, but I think a lot of those old fights and feelings are coming up again."

"Oh," I said. Then, "But . . . you like being Chinese, right?"

"Of course." Auntie Eva put her hand on mine. "Sorry, Cilla, I'm just tired and rambling. I love being Chinese. But there are lots of different ways to be Chinese. It's not about what any one person thinks."

"Huh," I said.

This was a lot to think about. I had lots of questions, but I didn't really know what they were. Or how to say them.

So, instead, I scooched closer and put my head on her shoulder, and she put her head on mine.

We sat there together, with our hot chocolate, and I could hear the kitchen clock ticking softly and the tree branches blowing in the wind outside.

And just sitting, and stepping back, and being quiet *was* nice, and I paid attention to so many other things, like how Auntie Eva's long white living room curtains swirl just a little where they touch the floor. And how Auntie Eva loves things that are simple and comfortable, like her giant fluffy white robe and her big chairs with giant pillows and the pile of blue-and-gray-striped blankets she keeps stacked neatly in the corner. And how Auntie Eva makes a tiny sigh whenever she sees something beautiful, like the branches of the trees against the sky when it began to turn to a light gray-yellow and blue.

And all of this was very nice to have seen.

Mom, Dad, and Gwendolyn came home and found us on the couch. We made dinner, sang "Happy Birthday" to Auntie Eva, and surprised her with a cake from her favorite bakery. It was the perfect ending to the day.

The next morning we went to a park and then to one of Auntie Eva's favorite Chinese restaurants. It was fun, though I got bored of all the talking about work, so I invented a game where I wrapped paper napkins around one of my chopsticks and dipped it in water. "Gross," Auntie Eva said. "It looks like earwax." I realized she was right, so I made up a song about it. It went:

Earwax on a stick!
Earwax on a stick!
You can't get your kicks without earwax on a stick!
It's mushy, it's gushy, it's really, really smushy!

Auntie Eva laughed and said, "Ewwwww!" And then, "Sing it again."

So I did. And she sang it too.

And every night on our vacation, Auntie Eva sat with me before bed and braided my hair and told me silly jokes and stories.

And I was very happy.

We could only spend the weekend at Auntie Eva's because she had to work. So we woke up early that Monday morning, and I got to see her in her work clothes, and they were AMAZING. She wore tall high heels and she had a briefcase that looked important and was packed full of papers.

"Goodbye, Cilla." She bent down and swung me up in a big hug, which was VERY impressive since she was doing it in high heels. "I can't wait to see you in June! We'll have so much fun, and you'll be my Special Wedding Helper, right? We'll go dress shopping with my mom together."

"YES!" I said. "I can't wait to see you too!" I hugged her back tightly.

My mom and dad said goodbye, and my dad said, "I love you, sis," and my mom said, "If you need me to distract your mom, just let me know. I'll make up a project for her."

Auntie Eva helped us get settled in the car, which took a few minutes because Gwendolyn had to be buckled and bags had to be put in the right places, and in the end I took out the bag with the snow globes for Colleen and Alien Face and put it on the seat next to me so they wouldn't be squished.

Then Auntie Eva stood on the porch steps and waved goodbye, and I waved and waved until I couldn't see her anymore.

I sat back and watched the trees and the buildings and the sky go by. And I pulled out the dinosaur snow globe and shook it to hear the water swish. I tried to watch, and to listen, and to not think about the fact that the next time I came here, Auntie Eva would be getting married. So Paul would live in her house too.

And I wondered if things would ever be like this again.

If Auntie Eva would still sit with me, and braid my hair, and play dinosaur and snow monster with me, and not care who saw.

I wondered if she would still have time for me, once she married Paul.

I think my mom noticed all the thoughts and worries on my face because suddenly she said, "Wow, look at those clouds, Cilla! I think I see one shaped like a duck—do you see it?"

"Yes," I said. "And there's one that looks like a cow!"

So we looked out the windows as our car sped along away from Auntie Eva, back toward home, and watched the sky go by.

DAISY, LIGHTNING,
AND OTHER CHALLENGES

Being perfect means you've done EVERY-
THING exactly right, which sounds great, even if
my dad does say I need to worry about it less
because it sometimes makes me upset.

I don't agree with him, though, because
shouldn't you want things to be perfect? And being
a little worried or upset seems worth it, if you get
everything you want in the end.

So, for example, it would be perfect if Gwendolyn found a destiny that made her special but also
not a writer. That's why I've been working hard,
since we've been back from break, to help her. So
far, I know she's not an architect, because when I
gave her blocks she just banged them together

instead of building a skyscraper. I also know she's not a musical genius, because when I put her at the electric keyboard, she just hit it with the blocks. And she's DEFINITELY not a cooking genius, because when I let her play with flour, she just threw it.

But even though all this trying is hard work (and made my dad say "argh" when he saw the mess in the kitchen), I know it will be worth it in the end.

Because then everything will be just the way it should be.

Sometimes, though, being perfect is hard in other ways.

Like on days like today. When *nothing* was the way I wanted it to be, and most frustrating of all, *I* wasn't the way I wanted to be.

The morning, at least, started off well because Colleen came over. We played, in this order:

1. Robots
2. Soccer Stars
3. Pillow Fort
4. Pillow Fort Part II, with fire-breathing sea-slug monsters
5. Pillow Fort Part III, with fire-breathing sea-slug monsters plus a princess

Pillow Fort Part II and III were especially fun, which was nice considering the fact that I'm trying to show Colleen that playdates at my house are the best things ever. And I was worried that our playdate wouldn't be perfect, since we have an unexpected guest.

A guest who is very loud, and snorty, and likes to charge and nip at people and things.

A guest who, I'll admit, makes a very convincing fire-breathing sea-slug monster.

Because this week, Daisy is staying at our house.

This wasn't a planned thing. But Grandma and Grandpa Jenkins are away on vacation, and there was a mix-up at the kennel right before they left, and my mom says this is What You Do for family. Daisy's been here a few nights now, and she sleeps in the kitchen and spends the rest of the day running around the house, trying to trip me, and snorting and nipping the whole time.

"She's really weird, isn't she?" Colleen asked as
we looked down at Daisy from behind the couch
pillows.

"Yeah," I said with a sigh. "She never slows
down. And when I bend to pick things up she
comes running and licks my nose and sometimes
knocks me over. I don't think I'd mind if she did it
in a friendly way, but it's all about food, because

then she chews at my fingers to see if I have anything to eat."

"Wow." Colleen shook her head. "Nothing like Spock."

"I know!" I said. "Spock's the PERFECT dog. I don't know what my grandparents were thinking."

Just then Daisy came running toward the fort pillows again, and Colleen said, "Attack! The slugs are attacking!"

And I said, "Oh no, protect the princess!"

And Gwendolyn said, "Pin-neh!" (Because she was the princess in our game. She seemed to really like this word, and it's a good one. But it's STILL not "Cilla.")

So we went back to playing.

Things were going really well, which was a relief considering that Daisy was there. Until right before Colleen had to go home.

"Cilla," she said, "I forgot to ask. My parents said I could bring a friend to the big soccer tournament at the end of the year. Do you want to come?

It'll be so much fun, and afterward, my mom and dad will take us to get ice cream and pizza to celebrate!"

I know what a big deal this is for Colleen—she's been talking about the soccer tournament for FOREVER. And I know she's nervous and excited, and it was really nice of her to invite me.

So I meant to say, "Yes! You're going to be amazing, and I can't wait to cheer for you!" Like a perfect best friend.

But I think my thoughts got ahead of me, and I wanted to be there, but I worried because what if the entire team was there too, and Melissa Hernandez, and would Colleen want to eat pizza and ice cream with them instead of me, and leave me all by myself with no one to talk to?

So instead, I said quickly, almost like I didn't care what the answer would be, "Well, will it be just us and no one else and special best-friend time?"

Colleen paused, and her forehead made a little

frown. And she got that funny look again, like she didn't know how to answer.

But then she said, "Sure." And then, "Is everything okay?"

And clearly, the answer was no, because every time Colleen plays with Melissa instead of me I get worried, and Alien-Face is still a little funny around me even though he really liked the snow globe, and I wish I could just tell Colleen my feelings.

But the perfect best friend is happy and fun all the time.

So I put on my biggest smile and said, "Of course! And I can't wait to cheer for you at the soccer game!"

Colleen looked happy, and the funny looks went away, and everything seemed fine again. Mostly.

Colleen's mom came a few minutes later. I waved goodbye as her car drove away, but Colleen didn't seem to wave back. And I didn't feel that great.

I was in a bad mood after that. Which made it worse when I found out that my Nai Nai and Ye Ye were coming over for dinner.

Which I usually LOVE.

But I knew *exactly* what would happen. And when the front door opened, I heard—

"Ay yah!" Nai Nai said as Daisy ran, jingling, around her feet. "Shoo."

I sighed, but I knew that there was nothing I could do.

"Ay yah," Nai Nai would say, every time Daisy ran through the room. And then, things like, "You let her in the kitchen?" Or, "So dirty."

And my mom would say, "She doesn't cause any trouble." (Which isn't true, but I see what my mom was going for.)

And my dad would say things like, "Ma, she's clean. Just try petting her." Or, "She's harmless, look how tiny she is."

But my Nai Nai just shook her head.

And when Ye Ye bent down and started to pet

her, Daisy began to nip at his fingers, and Nai Nai said, "Ay yah—careful, careful!" So Ye Ye stopped and didn't try to pet her again.

I knew this was a Tradition, like all the others.

So I tried to show them that I didn't like Daisy either.

I pretended I didn't see her when she ran around my feet, and I rolled my eyes when she started yapping, and I didn't scratch her ears after dinner, which I sometimes do (though quickly, and just in little pats, because of the whole finger-nipping thing).

And when we were done with dinner and Nai Nai offered to put Gwendolyn in her pajamas, I went to help and Daisy followed us. Nai Nai turned to look at her, at the door of Gwendolyn's nursery, and said, "Go away, dog," shaking her head. So I turned and said, "Yeah, go away, dog." And I shook my head too, and I closed the door behind us.

But I was surprised because all I could think

about was how Daisy had looked up at me with her big, round, oversized eyes.

And I felt bad.

Like there was no good choice at all.

Which didn't seem fair.

Tonight, when my mom was tucking me in, I asked, "Why did Grandma and Grandpa have to get a new dog?"

"Because," my mom said, "they wanted a change. It's good for them to have a dog. Your grandfather goes walking with Daisy every day, and your grandmother really enjoys the company while she grades papers. You know she stays by herself in the house for most of the day—when Grandpa goes to work, she goes to the office she keeps and works on her own projects. So it's nice that she has company. I think she's much happier now that Daisy's there."

"Oh," I said. "But"—I sighed—"but why *this* dog?

She's funny-looking, and she snorts, and she's embarrassing, and she's WEIRD. Why couldn't they get a regular, nice, *normal* dog that does normal dog things? Why does everything have to be so COMPLICATED?!"

"Cilla, sweetie," my mom said, "I know Daisy's a handful, but she can be fun, too. She just wants attention and needs a bit of training. I'm going to talk to your grandparents about it when they get back, actually—a puppy like Daisy needs more exercise than they're giving her. And she'll be going home before you know it." She saw my face and paused. "Is everything okay?" she asked.

"Yes," I grumbled, with my arms crossed. "I just HATE that dog."

"Well," my mom said, smoothing my hair back with her hand, "four more days."

Before she said good night, my mom read four whole chapters from *Selena Moon and the Curse of the Lunar Eclipse.*

Then she kissed me and turned off my lamp.

But I turned it back on because I couldn't sleep. So I'm writing.

And I'm frustrated because nothing is the way it should be.

Showing Colleen that I'm the best best friend EVER is actually really hard. Sometimes I wish that we could just go back to the way it used to be, so I didn't have to spend my playdates worrying that she's not having fun, or telling her everything is fine and not saying how I'm feeling.

And I want to make Nai Nai and Ye Ye happy. I want them to know that I love being Chinese. But it's sometimes hard to do that all the time. I didn't like hurting Daisy's feelings, even if she is strange and weird and kind of looks like a slug. And I didn't realize she means so much to my Grandma and Grandpa Jenkins. And I don't know how to be Chinese without hurting their feelings. And how do I tell Colleen how I feel without losing her to Melissa, and I'm mad at everyone, and there's just no way to make the perfect choices, and—

* * *

BOOM. Last night, I woke up, my notebook next to me and my pen by my pillow, where I'd fallen asleep writing.

BOOM. The sound of thunder was *everywhere*.

BOOM. The sky outside went white, and there was wind making a whistling sound, and I thought maybe the wind would break through my window, and I pulled the covers up over my face because I was scared.

Then I heard a new sound, from inside the house.

It was Daisy. She wasn't barking. She wasn't even snuffling or snorting. She was making a high sound.

A scared sound.

Daisy was *crying*.

It's okay, I told myself from under my covers. *Mom and Dad will wake up and know what to do. That's how things work.* But I didn't hear anything from their room, and the thunder *BOOMED* again. I couldn't get out of bed because it was scary and what if the window burst open and I didn't have my covers to protect me, and—

BOOM. I was up and out of my bed, even though I didn't really remember deciding to leave it, and running down the hallway to the kitchen.

"Daisy!" I yelled as I burst through the door.

A small inky-black shape raced toward me. And Daisy was in my arms.

"Shhhhh," I said. "Shhhhh, it's okay."

She pressed into me, shaking. I couldn't leave her there alone.

So I carried her, very carefully, back to my room.

I was still afraid of the window, even though the thunder was getting quieter now. So I sat on the floor, next to the bed, and I felt better having it there to protect me in case the wind and rain did get through. Daisy sat, the quietest and stillest she's ever been, in my lap, with her smushed-up nose pressed against my shoulder.

And together, we waited for the storm to end.

Daisy was warm and soft. I noticed how smooth her fur was and how her ears made perfect triangles. And the sound of her breathing was actually nice to hear. I listened to it go in and out, as the booming started to fade away. Until finally, it was gone.

When my room was quiet again, Daisy looked up at me and licked my nose once.

I made a decision.

"Get in, Daisy," I said as I dragged her dog bed from the kitchen into a corner of my room and climbed back into my bed. "Go to sleep." But she didn't and stood there on my rug, snuffling by the side of the bed, looking up at me.

"No, Daisy." I sighed. "You can't come up." I put my hand down to keep her from jumping up and felt something against my hand. "No, Daisy," I said again. But then I stopped and looked down. Daisy was curled up on the rug, her forehead pressed against my hand. Fast asleep.

So I closed my eyes too, and I felt Daisy's soft

fur, and I listened to her tiny snores as she breathed.

And that's how my dad found us when he came to get me in the morning.

My parents were sorry for not waking up and surprised that Gwendolyn didn't wake up during the storm (she's something called Fickle, which means she NEVER does what you think she will, and it's EXHAUSTING).

But it was okay, I told them.

Daisy and I had everything under control.

And that day, I began to notice new things about Daisy. Like how she loves being petted, and in fact, *that's* why she charges at you—because she's SO excited that you're petting her and worries you'll go away. So if you sit with her and keep petting her, she'll start to slow down, and she'll stop wriggling and nipping. And she'll sit with her eyes half-closed and breathe with her mouth open so it looks like a smile.

Though every once in a while she'll look up, snort, and lick your nose.

She's still Daisy, after all.

A few days later, I went to Nai Nai and Ye Ye's after school. After Nai Nai taught me some new Chinese words (I still haven't told her why I want to know them, which is hard, but surprises are worth it), Ye Ye and I sat at their small glass table and ate maan tau. Maan tau is white, fluffy Chinese bread, and we were practicing the best techniques for dipping it into dried pork (which is delicious). Behind us, Nai Nai was watching her Chinese soap operas, and beautiful women were walking around in fancy outfits, crying, as usual.

I'd just happened to glance back at the TV when—

"Wait," I gasped. "What is that?!!"

"Pekingese," Ye Ye said. "Traditional Chinese dog."

"But . . ." I looked wide-eyed at Ye Ye and then at Nai Nai. "But I thought Chinese people didn't like dogs," I said finally.

"Wah," Nai Nai said, looking up. "*I* just don't like dogs."

I looked at her with big eyes.

"There weren't many dogs," she explained, "where I was growing up. And when I was little, a dog bite me. I don't like them now."

"Oh," I said again. And then, "So . . . Chinese people can like dogs too?"

Ye Ye laughed. "Of course. You know, Daisy, your grandparents' dog, is a Chinese dog. Pugs were originally Chinese pets."

This was a lot to take in.

"You know, Nai Nai," I said, after a minute, "Daisy is actually really nice. She wouldn't ever hurt you—she kept me company during a lightning storm when I was scared, and when Gwendolyn pulled her tail yesterday, she didn't even bark."

"Hmmmmm," Nai Nai said. But in a different way than usual.

And right before Grandma and Grandpa Jenkins came back from their trip, Nai Nai and Ye Ye came over for dinner again.

Nai Nai laughed when she saw how Daisy followed me around (she even sits outside the bathroom door when I'm inside). And when Nai Nai thought no one was looking, I saw her bend down and give Daisy a quick pat on the head.

But just once.

We sat on the couch after dinner, and Daisy jumped in my lap, like she always does now.

"Wah," Ye Ye said. "She loves you."

"Really?" I asked, not sure if I believed him.

"Of course," he said. "Just look at her."

Daisy snorted, probably because she knew we were talking about her.

So I looked down at her looking up at me, and at her big bug eyes and that squished, snuffling nose. She was nothing at all like Spock. The perfect dog.

"You," I told her, "are really weird."

Then I gave her a kiss on her wrinkled forehead.

She licked my nose.

As if she agreed.

And it didn't matter at all.

BURGER PLANET-AH

When you speak Chinese and you use English words or names in your sentences, you add an "ah" to the end. I don't know why this is—it's just a rule. So sometimes when my dad speaks in Chinese with my Nai Nai or Ye Ye because he doesn't want me to know what he's saying, it doesn't work. Because even though I don't speak Chinese, I hear "Cilla-ah" and "ice cream-ah" and I know where we're going and get really excited. This also means that my dad calls my Ye Ye "Daddy-ah," when he speaks in Chinese, which I think is the best thing EVER.

This is why I was REALLY excited when my Ye Ye called my dad a few days ago. I was sitting right next to him at the kitchen table, and through the phone I heard first "Cilla-ah" and then "Roller Kingdom-ah,"

So I was already bouncing up and down in my chair and clapping my hands when my dad turned to me and said, "Your Ye Ye wants to know if you want to go to Roller Kingdom this weekend."

And I said, "YES!" because Roller Kingdom is an arcade and a roller-skating rink that's inside, and they play music and there are different-colored lights everywhere, and there's nothing better for the imagination (and fun) than that.

Through the phone, I could hear Ye Ye say something else in Chinese, and my dad said, "Great! Cilla, Ye Ye says you can bring a friend to Roller Kingdom too."

"Oh," I said. I do a lot of things with my Ye Ye, but I've never gone on a playdate when he was there.

"How about Colleen?" my mom asked as she fed Gwendolyn across the table. "You two love roller-skating together, right?"

"Right," I said.

But when I called Colleen, she had a soccer game and couldn't go.

"I guess it will just be me and Ye Ye," I said.

"Well," my mom said, trying to clean off Gwendolyn, who was done eating and now using her spoon to make drumming noises (though I don't think she's a future drumming legend, because she doesn't like when things are loud). "Why don't you ask Ben? I'm sure he'd love to come."

"Um," I said. "I mean . . ." I paused. "It's just that we've never had a playdate just the two of us before, and he doesn't really know Ye Ye."

"Well, he met Ye Ye at your last birthday party," my mom pointed out.

"Okay," I said. But I was kind of nervous when I called Alien-Face's house to ask because this wasn't how things usually are. And even though he'd loved the dinosaur snow globe, things still seemed kind of funny with him. Sometimes, when Colleen wasn't playing kickball, he wouldn't come over to play with us on the playground, like he thought we didn't want to see him. Which was sad.

But he sounded happy when I called, and he said he'd love to come. So it all seemed okay, even though, as Saturday got closer, I felt kind of funny and sort of wished it was just me and Ye Ye. Because special playdates like this are usually with Colleen. It felt strange to go with someone else. Plus Colleen has had Chinese food with me and met my Nai Nai and Ye Ye and knows what tzuck sang and maan tau are. But she's the only friend who's ever done those things.

And I wondered if Alien-Face would think these things were weird.

Or if he thought I wasn't Chinese enough to do them.

We picked Alien-Face up at his house, and in the car, Ye Ye asked him about his helmet and the alligator stickers on it. Then we talked about fancy roller-skating tricks, and Alien-Face said he's an expert twirler. So I said I was an expert skate-on-one-leg-er (this wasn't really true, because I'd never tried it before, but it seemed like a fun idea). And Ye Ye said he was an expert roller-skating high-fiver, which I hadn't known before.

When we got to the rink, Ye Ye went to rent us skates.

"Your grandpa's really nice," Alien-Face said.

"Thanks," I said.

"I was confused, though," he went on, "because when you called, you said your grandpa was taking you roller-skating, so I'd thought we were going with your other grandpa—the one who wears a bow tie. You don't call this grandpa 'Grandpa,' right?"

"Well, no. . . ." I took a deep breath. "I call him the Chinese word for 'Grandpa.' Which is 'Ye Ye,'" I said, saying the last part quickly.

"How do you say it again?" he asked.

"Ye Ye," I said. And he repeated it.

"Perfect," I said, impressed.

"Great!" he said. "Also, did you see the dinosaur sticker I put on the back of my helmet?"

Suddenly, I felt better.

And *very* excited to roller-skate.

We put on our skates and our helmets, and it turns out that Alien-Face's mom makes him wear elbow pads and kneepads too, so I didn't feel funny about wearing mine at all.

Ye Ye is REALLY good at making turns, and he IS an expert at high-fiving whenever we skate by. And Alien-Face twirled, and we made up a game where you did different dares (but you could say no, and they had to be safe, Ye Ye said). So we'd dare each other to try to skate backward or to skate on one leg, and it was all very fun.

And when I fell and Ye Ye said, "Ay yah!" Alien-Face didn't seem to mind.

We skated for a loooong time, and we didn't want to leave. But Ye Ye said it was getting late, plus were we hungry? (The answer to that was "yes!")

"What would you like to eat?" Ye Ye asked as he helped us to buckle into our seats. "I saw a lot of restaurants on our way here—there's sushi, and a pizza restaurant, and something called Burger Planet."

Alien-Face and I both gasped.

"Burger Planet!" we said.

"Wah!" Ye Ye said. "So excited! What's Burger Planet?"

"It's the best place EVER," I said. "It has burgers with a secret special sauce that they only make there, and French fries and chocolate milk shakes, and a playground inside, though that's for little kids. But Mom NEVER lets me go."

"Mine neither," Alien-Face said. "Which is ridiculous, because the commercials always say that everyone can find something to love at Burger Planet. So my parents would definitely like it too."

"Exactly!" I said. "*Everyone* loves Burger Planet. Please, Ye Ye?" I asked, clasping my hands together under my chin and giving him my biggest smile.

"Yes, please, Ye Ye?" Alien-Face also gave him his biggest smile and put his hands under his chin, just like I did.

Ye Ye laughed. "Okay, but only if it isn't too far. I'll call your dad for directions."

Alien-Face and I clapped our hands and cheered.

Ye Ye called, and I heard "Burger Planet-ah." And even though Alien-Face had thought "Ye Ye" was a neat name, I hoped that he wasn't paying attention, in case he thought Chinese sounded funny. (Not paying attention is a BIG Theme with Alien-Face, because he gets distracted A LOT, especially during math.) But apparently that only applies to school. "Burger Planet-ah?" he asked. "Why does he say it like that?"

"That's just what you do in Chinese," I said quietly. "You add 'ah' to the end of English words."

"Huh," he said. "So what game should we play in the car?"

And I smiled. Because car games are always excellent.

By the time Ye Ye got the directions, Alien-Face and I were still trying to come up with a new game. So Ye Ye dared us to chant "Burger Planet" and not stop until we got there.

"No!" Alien-Face said suddenly. "We should chant Burger Planet-ah!"

"*YES*," I said.

And we did.

Though by the time we got there, I think Ye Ye wished he'd picked a different dare.

Burger Planet has brightly colored booths, and you order at a long counter. I wasn't going to order the special kids' Out of This World Box (which has food *plus* a toy inside). I didn't want Alien-Face to laugh at me, since we're going to be fourth graders soon and too big for special kids' meals. So I tried to ignore the big display of all the toys they have.

Until I saw Alien-Face also looking at them out of the corner of his eye.

"I'll get an Out of This World Box if you will," I said.

"*YES*," he said.

Then Ye Ye said we could also get chocolate milk shakes, and it was pretty much the best thing ever.

Ye Ye carried all our food over on a tray to one of the booths and made sure we had everything we needed. He raised an eyebrow when he realized the burger was wrapped in paper. But then he shrugged and took a bite.

"This is delicious!" he said, surprised. "What is this sauce? I have to take your Nai Nai here."

I giggled and then explained that "Nai Nai" was the Chinese word for "Grandma" before Alien-Face even had to ask.

We were all tired by the time Ye Ye drove us home, so Ye Ye put on some pretty music. Alien-Face and I started talking about the third-grade relay race, which is happening just next week.

"I think our class will do a good job," he said.

"Especially because we have all the people who do sports, like John and Yuki and Melvin, though I don't think he can play basketball right now with his broken arm. But he's a pretty good runner. And then we have Colleen and Melissa. Did you know Melissa's supposed to be *really* good at soccer?" he asked.

"Hmmm," I said, pressing my lips together. "I didn't."

Alien-Face gave me a funny look.

"Why don't you like Melissa?" he asked after a minute.

"Well," I said slowly. "It's not that I don't like her. It's just that I don't think she likes me, and she never talks to me, and she's always whispering to Colleen and giggling. And, well . . . I think she's Plotting to take Colleen away, and to make Colleen her best friend instead of mine." I said the last part very quickly, and I waited for him to gasp because Evil Plots are *very* Dramatic.

But Alien-Face McGee *laughed*.

"She's not Plotting," he said. "She's just shy."

"What?!" I turned to stare at him. "No, she's not. She just doesn't like me."

"Nooooo," Alien-Face said slowly. "She's just shy. That's why she's so quiet all the time. And Colleen's really nice to her, and she's really good at making people feel like they can talk. You know that," he said, like it was the most obvious thing in the world. "You're her best friend."

All I could do was blink. I waited for a sign that Alien-Face was joking or making things up.

But I didn't see any.

We were quiet for a minute after that.

I thought about Alien-Face McGee, sitting by the window across from me.

And all the things he'd noticed—about Melissa, and about Colleen, the person I'm supposed to know the best.

I thought about all the things that I hadn't noticed or paid attention to.

And suddenly, I wasn't thinking about Colleen, or even Melissa, anymore.

"I'm sorry," I said, softly, looking at the seat in front of me, "that I hurt your feelings at recess. I don't play with you just because Colleen isn't there. I play with you because it's fun. Because you're a really good friend."

"Thanks," Alien-Face said quietly. "You're a good friend too." And then he grinned. "Also, this day has been the BEST. Next time, you should come over to my house, and we can make snow cones with my dad's machine."

"YES," I said.

And, suddenly, there was *a lot* to talk about again.

On Monday, Colleen said, "Cilla!" when I got on the bus, like she always does. "What did you do this weekend? Did you go to Roller Kingdom with your Ye Ye?"

"Yes," I said, bouncing up and down, because Colleen would LOVE my Roller Kingdom stories, and I opened my mouth to tell her and then . . . I stopped.

"Um . . . ," I said. Suddenly, I didn't know what to say, and I realized that I was getting funny and blinking a lot.

Like Colleen had been doing with me.

All because I *didn't want to hurt Colleen's feelings.*

"Um," I said again. "Well, I did go to Roller Kingdom. And then to Burger Planet. But, since you couldn't come, um, Alien-Face did instead."

"Oh," Colleen said. And she blinked and crossed her arms and was quiet for a minute. "So, what skating tricks did you guys do?" she asked. Her voice was fast and funny, like she didn't care.

"Just some ones we made up," I said. I wondered if she was mad at me.

"Did you make up games in the ball pit, like we always do?" she asked in that same voice. "Were his games more fun than mine?"

And it all made sense.

Colleen was jealous. Just like I was jealous of

Melissa. And maybe she worried that Alien-Face would be my best friend, and she wouldn't anymore.

But I knew, all of a sudden, that that's not how it works.

I reached out and put my hand on her shoulder.

"No one can be you, Colleen," I said.

Slowly, her arms uncrossed, and she put a hand on mine.

"Thanks, Cilla," she said, her normal Colleen-voice back. "No one can be you, either."

The bus rolled on, and we sat there, talking and laughing about our weekends, and soccer, and Burger Planet.

Two best friends.

A few days later, Ye Ye *did* **take Nai Nai to** Burger Planet, just like he'd said he would.

Nai Nai said the hamburgers were cooked too much.

But she liked the French fries. And the special sauce.

Which makes sense.

Because there are some things that everyone can understand. Like how great roller-skating is, and new games and fun times with your Ye Ye. And even getting a little jealous when your friends make new ones. And how you have to learn that just because they make new friends, it doesn't mean they're not yours anymore.

And of course, that everyone can find something to love at Burger Planet-ah.

9

TEAMWORK ISN'T (ALL THAT) BAD

Usually I don't really like teamwork.

The idea of it is nice, of course. But in school, whenever a teacher says "teamwork," you know it means there's going to be a project with lots of other kids, and sometimes these can be fun (when they're with Colleen or Alien-Face, for example), but sometimes they're stressful (when you're with Tim #2 or John Mulligan, for example, because they'll just be silly and then you have to do their work for them).

Or teamwork comes up in gym class when it comes to things like kickball, and I think we've already covered my feelings on kickball.

So I was NOT looking forward to the big third-grade relay race, with all the third-grade classes competing against each other.

Because Mr. Flight said it was all about class spirit and teamwork, and everyone knows what that means.

The morning of the race, I wondered if I could pretend I was sick. But that didn't work, and my mom just said, "Let's go, Young Lady," when I told her I might be getting a cold or pneumonia or the bubonic plague so should probably stay home to be safe.

Then, when Mr. Flight said, "Okay—it's time!" I wondered if I could pretend to faint or trip and say my leg was broken or falling off.

But Colleen was next to me bouncing up and down and saying, "I'm so excited!" So the next thing I knew, I was outside.

There were A LOT of students on the field because we have three third-grade classrooms, each with a team name that the teachers had picked out for us—Mr. Flight's Falcons, Ms. Scofield's Sea Horses, and Mr. Garabaldi's Gerbils. These were GREAT names, so at least there was *something* good about this race, I told myself.

Ms. Gladden, our gym teacher, got up on a crate to start organizing the race. Even though I don't like gym, I love Ms. Gladden—she's funny and strong, and she likes to use BIG and fancy terms like "brave souls," and "the victors" and "a test of agility," which I usually appreciate because they add Drama. But when Ms. Gladden started using words like these that morning, they actually just made my stomach feel even more fluttery.

"All right, third graders," Ms. Gladden shouted. "Are you ready for the big one, the stuff of legends, the third-grade RELAY RACE?!" Everyone cheered so I tried to cheer too, but I didn't do that great a job. Which is too bad because a legend is a type of Classic, so I should have been cheering loudest of all.

"Okay, here are the rules," Ms. Gladden went on. "Every orange cone on the field marks a different activity. The first class to complete all activities and to make it across the finish line in the final frog-jumping dash will win."

Tim #2, who loves sports, said, "Awesome!"

"Are you ready, third graders?" Ms. Gladden shouted.

And John Mulligan jumped up and down and said, "I was born ready."

He and Tim #2 were smiling, and lots of the third graders were looking excited.

"Now, to start," Ms. Gladden said, "I'm going to tell you about all the activities, and I'll give you a chance to volunteer for the game you'll compete in. There's going to be a little bit of everything—racing, basketball, even some soccer." ("Yes!" I heard Colleen whisper next to me.)

I tried to smile for her, but it was hard because I'm not good at ANY of those things.

"We'll have some activities where we'll double

up, so everyone gets a chance," Ms. Gladden explained. "But *every student* will need to participate in *at least one* activity. And I want to hear LOTS of cheering. Remember, a good team sticks together, because *everyone* contributes to the win."

And I swear that I heard John Mulligan say, "Yeah, right," and I saw him roll his eyes and look at Melvin and his giant (AMAZING, bright green) cast. And I thought I saw other skeptical looks too, and saw a few people look my way, and already I knew that Ms. Gladden was wrong. I would NOT make a good team member, and no one wanted to stick together if it meant having me play. So I tried to make myself smaller where I stood.

Ms. Gladden came to sort us into activities, class by class, starting with ours.

"Now, to begin," she said, "we'll need three brave souls to compete in the opening zigzagged relay."

"Me, me!" I saw Tim #2, John Mulligan, Lina Mirza, and a few other kids raising their hands, because they love running.

"Lina, John, and Tim," Ms. Gladden said.

"Then," she continued, "there's the basketball bog challenge. In this race, you'll need to make five shots before moving on to the next round." Melvin sighed and looked unhappily at the ground, and she picked Jeannie Kishi and Becky Davidow.

The list of activities went on and on. Colleen volunteered for soccer ball kicking, Alien-Face volunteered for the balance beam race, and Melissa volunteered for the final frog-jumping dash. And Melvin kept sighing because Ms. Gladden said he couldn't do the balance beams or anything with jumping, because he might fall and hurt his arm.

We were getting toward the end, and there weren't many activities left, and I wondered if maybe Ms. Gladden would make an exception and not make us all participate, because everyone knew I would NOT be contributing to the win. I could see Melvin also looking kind of nervous, and John was saying, "Can I do three things? I'll win them all!" And I wondered if there would be something for me, and—

Then Ms. Gladden said, "Now, in the second-to-last activity, I'll need two brave souls from each class to participate in . . . the chopstick race!"

"Huh," I said.

"You will have to make it across half the field, racing as you hold a peeled grape in a pair of chopsticks," Ms. Gladden went on. "Then, you will pass the grape off to your teammate, using only your chopsticks, and your teammate will finish the race. But if the grape is dropped at any point, *both* runners will have to start again at the other side of the field."

"Wow," Tim #2 said, "that's hard."

"Wait." Melvin looked at me. "That's all?"

"I . . . I think so?" I said. Melvin looked at his cast hand, wiggled his fingers, and grinned.

"So, any volunteers?" Ms. Gladden asked.

Melvin and I looked at each other. Then, together, we raised our hands.

"I was born ready," Melvin said.

"Yeah." I nodded. "Me too."

The other classrooms were sorted into activities,

and soon, Ms. Gladden was blowing her whistle, and we went to take our places. I followed Melvin toward our spot in the field. Just behind me was Melissa, who would be starting the final frog-jumping run close by us.

She didn't look like she wanted to talk.

So I almost kept going, staying just ahead of her.

But I remembered what Alien-Face McGee had said.

And I noticed her frowning look. The one she has anytime she has to give a book report in front of the class, or share her work with the table.

So I slowed down, and in a moment, we were walking side by side.

"You're going to be great at the dash," I said.

"Really?" She looked at me, surprised.

"Yeah," I said. "I've seen you play hopping games at recess. You're *so* fast."

"Thanks." She tried to smile but didn't quite lose that worried look. "I just wish there weren't so many people watching. Having other people around can make me really nervous sometimes. I'm kind of shy. I even get scared before every soccer game."

"I didn't know that," I said. And then, "You know . . . I'm shy too."

"What?!" Melissa actually stopped walking. "But," she said, "but it seems like you *always* know what to say."

"Wow," I said. That was a BIG compliment. "Thank you." I grinned.

"I never know what to say," Melissa went on. "And sometimes I really want to tell someone what I think or want, and I just *can't*."

"I know what you mean," I said. "And then I get even madder at myself because I wish I'd said something, so I just keep feeling bad all around."

"*Yes*," she said. "Though . . . well, I'm not as good with words as you are. I could never make up stories like yours, and I'd *never* be able to tell them to other people. I'd be too scared."

"Well . . . ," I said. "But you go out and play

soccer games, in front of all those people, even though it scares you. That's so BRAVE. I could never, ever do that."

"Really?" she asked.

"Really," I said.

From the other side of the field, we heard Ms. Gladden yelling, "Okay, third graders, time to get into place!"

"You're going to be great," I said.

And I don't know which one of us was more surprised, because I reached out and I *hugged* Melissa Hernandez.

"Good luck," I said.

"Good luck," she said, hugging me back.

And we went to take our places for the third-grade relay race.

* * *

Melvin and I waited at our spots, chopsticks
in hand. He was at the starting line that Ms. Gladden had made with cones, and I was halfway across
the field, in a line with third graders from the
other classes. The rule was that you couldn't go
until a teammate from the game before tagged
you. When he was tagged, Melvin would race to the
bowl where the grapes were kept, pick one up with
his chopsticks, and then run across the field as fast
as he could to me, where we could hand off the
grape with "no hands, no spearing the grape, just
chopsticks!" Ms. Gladden had shouted this with
a stern look. Then I would run to the other end
of the field, drop the grape in a bowl, and tag
Melissa, who would finish the race.

I was nervous, but I was excited, too, and the
kids from the other classes also seemed nervous.
We smiled at each other, and then we cheered as
the race began.

"Colleeeeeeeeeen!" I yelled REALLY loudly so

she could hear me, because she was doing an EXCELLENT job. It was fun to watch, and when Alien-Face McGee fell off the balance beam and had to start the run over again, the kids from the other classes were really nice to him. And they were impressed because when he got back on the beam, he was so fast that he still came in second place.

John had also tripped at the beginning of the

race and set our team back a little. But Colleen was such a good soccer kicker, and Tim #1 was such a good Hula-Hooper, that by the time the hopscotch was happening, which was the race before mine, Mr. Flight's Falcons had caught up with Ms. Scofield's Sea Horses.

"Yay!" we cheered, as Sasha leaped through the hopscotch race. Other kids, who were done with their activities, had run down to our end of the field and were cheering Sasha on. And Sasha took the lead, but the girl from Ms. Scofield's Sea Horses was just a bit faster. She cleared the finish line, and all her classmates were cheering as she tagged the boy next to Melvin.

But Sasha wasn't far behind, and she ran forward and yelled, "Go, Melvin, go!" He ran to the bowl where the other boy was still fumbling to pick up the grape. Melvin reached in with his bright green arm and, without banging the other boy's chopsticks, grabbed a grape. Then he was running toward me!

"Go, Melvin!" I yelled.

He was almost to me, and the boy from Ms. Scofield's Sea Horses was right behind him. Melvin reached out, and I reached out, and I grabbed the grape from right between his chopsticks. Then I was running, and I saw out of the side of my eye that the boy from Ms. Scofield's was having trouble passing the grape to his partner. The girl from Mr. Garabaldi's Gerbils had dropped her grape and was sprinting back to the starting line, and the boy behind me was catching up. From the side of the field I heard Colleen's voice yelling, "Go, Cilla! You're almost there!" she yelled.

"Yay, Cilla!" Melvin and Alien-Face and Sasha yelled together.

I squeezed my chopsticks tightly and sped up, and suddenly the grape was in the bowl. I dashed toward Melissa, who was waiting for me. She yelled, "Amazing, Cilla!" I lunged forward and touched her hand, and she was OFF.

There was no time to stop. I followed Colleen and the rest of our classmates.

"Come on, Melissa!" we yelled.

The boy racing behind Melissa leaped forward— but not before a whistle blew, and Melissa WON THE FROG-JUMPING RACE.

"The champions!" Ms. Gladden yelled. "Mr. Flight's Falcons!"

"Yay!!!" And then we were jumping and hugging, and we all ran up to Melissa, and she hugged Colleen, and then me, which made Colleen look really surprised and then really happy.

I'd dropped my chopsticks in the field in all the excitement, so I went to get them (because littering is bad). Melvin was there too, getting his pair, and we high-fived with his unbroken arm, and he said, "Good job, team." And I said, "Good job, team," back, because that was a *great* line.

As we walked toward the school building, I saw Colleen, Alien-Face, and Melissa walking with their arms linked. They were smiling and laughing and happy, and Melissa was talking and laughing too, along with everyone else.

And it was a really, really nice thing to see.

Everything seemed almost perfect.

Until Alien-Face turned back to me and yelled, "Come on, Silly, if you don't hurry, I'll eat your Popsicle!"

I smiled and said, "Oh, no you won't!"

And then I said, "Come on, Melvin!"

And we ran to join them.

That afternoon we had a class party, and all our parents came. Colleen's mom and dad gave me a hug, and Colleen's mom said, "I can't believe you're going to be fourth graders!" Alien-Face's mom took pictures of us all, and his dad made funny jokes about how Colleen will be taller than him any day now (this might actually be true—she *is* getting pretty tall). We all had a great time, even though I think maybe my mom's catching a cold because she kept wiping her nose on the colorful napkins

Mr. Flight had brought in for cake. I also got to meet Melissa's mom and dad, and I think my mom and Melissa's mom are going to be friends too.

Mr. Flight made a speech to our parents, and he said something nice about each of us and made me promise to send him autographed copies of all my future bestselling books. And Harold sang a song halfway through Mr. Flight's speech, which I think was his way of saying we're great, and he'll miss us.

Just as the afternoon was coming to an end, Colleen and I started talking about the weekend and the soccer tournament.

"It's going to be AMAZING," Colleen said. "Everyone who plays will get a special T-shirt, and my parents said we could get pizza, milk shakes, *and* ice cream after the game."

"That does sound amazing," I said. And then, "Colleen, did . . . did you want to invite Melissa to the party after the tournament too? I mean—I know she's your friend. And it might be nice to celebrate together."

Colleen looked uncertain.

"You won't mind?" she asked.

"No." I smiled. "It'll be fun."

"That would be great," she said. "And actually . . . my parents said we could still make it a bigger party, if we want. So, what if Alien-Face came too? You could cheer together, and besides, pizza parties are his favorite."

"Perfect," I said.

The game was nothing short of Epic, which is another kind of Classic Story. Alien-Face and I made up cheerleading chants, and we could barely talk when it was over, we'd been yelling so much. Colleen and Melissa were an amazing team together, and even though I knew that Melissa was scared beforehand, you couldn't tell at all. Especially with Colleen there, who during the game kept yelling things like, "Good job, Melissa!" and "Over here, Melissa!" and "Nice kick, Melissa!"

And in between my cheering, I remembered how Colleen and I had met each other, when I was too shy to talk to anyone in kindergarten. But Colleen had asked me to tell her a story, and she was nice and friendly and encouraging, so I forgot all about my shyness, and it made school great.

I watched her with Melissa, doing all those same things, the things that make her my best friend in all the world.

And I was very proud of her.

I had a chance to tell her too, at our pizza party, where we made up all kinds of games, like who can find the most unusual way to eat their pizza (Melissa won, because she folded hers up and took bites like when you make a paper snowflake, and then her pizza slice had polka-dot holes in it).

Next year, I'll be in fourth grade. I won't find out until the summer if I'll be in the same class with Colleen, or Alien-Face, or Melissa. But I hope I will.

And even if I'm not, I know that it will be okay.

We're Mr. Flight's Falcons, after all. And on our last day of third grade, Mr. Flight said that we'd been one of the best classes he'd ever had, with some of the strongest friendships he'd ever seen, and that it had made him so happy that—and then he did a BACKFLIP!

Because Mr. Flight has an EXCELLENT flair for Drama, which I really understand and appreciate.

Even if he still can't fly.

10

BRIDAL SHOWERS AREN'T ACTUALLY ABOUT SHOWERING

Auntie Eva came to stay with us right as school ended to do all the final preparations for the wedding. For the first few days, though, you almost couldn't tell that she was here. In fact, Daisy was staying with us too (Grandma and Grandpa Jenkins were away for the weekend), and I spent *way* more time with her. Auntie Eva got up early and went to bed early too, so there was no hair braiding or sitting up late together. (Though Daisy sat up with me and slept by the side of my mini-tent. It was nice, but not the same.)

But I understood why Auntie Eva was so busy. There was A LOT to do, and Auntie Eva and Nai Nai spent entire days looking at things like plates and tablecloths, and arguing over whether or not Auntie Eva needs a complete Chinese tea set (Auntie Eva won) or a rice cooker (Nai Nai won, which I'm glad about, because rice is the best).

But finally, it was the day I'd been waiting for—our special Dress Shopping day, when I'd get to spend the *entire* day with Auntie Eva.

Dress Shopping is Serious Business, apparently. Grandma Jenkins says it's important to make a good First Impression at weddings and that clothes can make all the difference. And she and my mom both got *beautiful* new dresses for the wedding—Grandma's is light green with white flowers at the top, and my mom's is bright blue, with a big flowy skirt. And my mom said, "Great dress, Mom. Y'know, I just don't think it needs that hat...." Because she HATES Grandma Jenkins's Special Occasions hat, which is made of white straw and HUGE. Though I love it, no matter how "ridiculous" my mom says it is, because it's very Dramatic and in a good way this time.

But Grandma said, "Nonsense, dear. This dress

will go perfectly. I'm going to order a flower to pin to the hat, white with green leaves, just like the colors of the dress, to tie them together. And at this new shop I've found, you'd never be able to tell that the flowers are plastic. . . ."

Which shows just how seriously Grandma Jenkins takes First Impressions.

When I went shopping with Auntie Eva and Nai Nai, though, there were no hats. First I found a bright red dress, which I thought Nai Nai would look AMAZING in, plus red is for good luck. But Nai Nai and Auntie Eva said no, and Nai Nai said that in Chinese weddings, only the bride wears red, which makes *another* Tradition I had no idea about.

But it didn't take long after that for Nai Nai to find the *perfect* dress. It's long and flowy and a light purple color, with silver thread sewn in the shapes of flowers and swirls at the bottom.

When Nai Nai came out of the dressing room, Auntie Eva clapped and said, "Mom! You look wonderful!"

I said, "Wow, Nai Nai. You look beautiful."

And Nai Nai giggled and said, "Don't sound so surprised." Which was funny.

After we found Nai Nai's dress and then a purse and shoes to go with it, it was finally, after *months* of waiting, my turn. We dropped Nai Nai off at our house because she wanted to rest, and we picked up my mom and Gwendolyn. All together we went to try on my FLOWER GIRL DRESS.

"It was the easiest decision in the whole wedding!" Auntie Eva said. "You're going to love it!"

We went into the fanciest dressing room I've ever been in, with mirrors everywhere. Auntie Eva held Gwendolyn while my mom came in with me, unzipped a bag hanging from a rack, and pulled out the most BEAUTIFUL dress I've EVER SEEN. It was white, just like I'd thought it would be, and it was even poofier than I'd imagined (which I hadn't really thought was possible). There was lace all down the skirt, and the top was satiny and smooth, and there was a tiny little rose by one shoulder. My mom slipped the dress over my head and zipped me up, and it was waaaaay too long, but she said that was an easy fix. We opened the door to show Auntie Eva.

"Cilla," she said, clapping her hands. "You look beautiful!"

"Thank you," I said.

"Bah-man!" Gwendolyn said, also clapping. So then Auntie Eva got her Batman toy out of the diaper bag and made him fly around while Gwendolyn giggled. And Gwendolyn wasn't interested AT ALL in the pinning going on, so I crossed future fashion designer off the list of potential Destinies.

Pinning dresses takes a while. So I had a chance to look around, and then to look at myself in the mirror. The store was big and fancy. Everything was gleaming and clean, and the walls were covered with pictures of brides, bridesmaids, and flower girls, laughing and confident, with no one seeming nervous.

And my stomach did a flip as I looked in the mirror at my always-messy hair and still-too-long dress. I remembered Paul and his perfect family,

who pose for perfect photos. And I wondered what I would look like when I was standing next to them.

But my mom saw my expression and squeezed my hand and said, "You look beautiful, sweetheart. And your aunt's so happy that you can be a part of the ceremony. She was telling me how much it means to her to have you there."

I smiled and squeezed her hand back.

Because messy hair or not, it was still nice to hear.

Auntie Eva and I were tired because it had been a LOOOOONG day of dresses. So my mom drove home, dropped us off outside our house, and went on to the grocery store with Gwendolyn to get a few things for the family dinner we were having before the Bridal Shower the next day.

The house seemed quiet and still, and I thought Nai Nai was still resting. So we didn't yell out to say we were home or think to look for Nai Nai.

Which is why we were both VERY surprised when we rounded the corner to the kitchen and found Nai Nai sitting on the floor.

And there, on her lap, was *Daisy*, snorting happily as Nai Nai stroked her soft, silky ears with the tips of her fingers.

"Mom!" Auntie Eva said, sounding as surprised as I felt. "I didn't know you liked dogs."

"I don't like *dogs*," Nai Nai said, frowning as she stroked Daisy's ears. "I like THIS dog."

"Nai Nai!" I sighed happily. "That was AMAZING Precision of Language."

Nai Nai smiled, and Daisy snorted and licked her nose and then ran over to me to say hello.

The next day, we had the Bridal Shower, the last Big Event before we'd see Auntie Eva at her wedding.

The Shower was a big party at our house because lots of Auntie Eva's friends from when she was little live near us. It was a little confusing at first, and I had to put away my bathing suit after my mom cleared up the whole shower thing (I'm still working on understanding expressions—some of them are very strange).

But it was a *really* fun party. There were lots of people there, and I even got to meet Auntie Eva's maid of honor, her best friend, Jane. I can tell why Jane is Auntie Eva's best friend. She loves to laugh and tells excellent jokes, and when lots of people were talking to Auntie Eva all at once, she pushed through them and made sure that Auntie Eva had had a chance to eat.

Which is the sign of an EXCELLENT best friend. And that's a BIG compliment coming from me, because my standards are very high.

There were *games* at the Bridal Shower too, which was unexpected but great. We were put in teams and had to dress someone up in wedding dresses that we made out of rolls of toilet paper, and by the end, Jane looked like a mummy because we wrapped her in so much.

Through it all there was talking and laughing, and Lucy, the pretty woman who Nai Nai calls "Jane's best friend" and Auntie Eva calls "Jane's girlfriend" laughed and took pictures with her giant camera. And even though I didn't get to see Auntie Eva that much, because there were so many people, I still had a great time.

That night, I went down to my mini-tent to go to sleep, and my mom and dad came and kissed me good night. But I couldn't sleep. I sat down by the couch to read but didn't want to do that either. So I looked off, thinking, and I didn't notice the sound of someone coming down the stairs until . . .

"Hey, stranger," Auntie Eva said. "Am I bothering you?"

"No," I said.

She sat down on the floor next to me, leaning against the couch, and put an arm around me.

"Things have been so busy," she said. "I just wanted to see you before I leave tomorrow. Want me to braid your hair before you go to bed?"

"Yes, please." I smiled.

We sat together as she braided. Just me and Auntie Eva. Like we've always been.

"You seemed kind of quiet tonight," she said as she smoothed my hair back from my face. "Is everything okay?"

"Yeah," I said, softly.

"Your mom told me you were kind of nervous."

"Yeah," I said again.

"Well, you're going to be great," she said. "Paul's so excited to meet you. And his family is so nice. I think you'll really like his cousins. They're about your age."

"That does sound nice," I said, smiling. And then, in a quieter voice, "I'm excited to meet Paul too."

I looked up and saw Auntie Eva smiling as she braided.

So I was happy I'd said it.

Even if that wasn't really what I felt.

Because I couldn't stop thinking about Paul's family. His Very Impressive, High-Powered, perfect Chinese family.

I imagined them all speaking the same language, and knowing the same Traditions, and eating with the chopsticks that waiters set out for them whenever they walked in.

And even though Auntie Eva said that there are lots of ways to be Chinese, I'm not so sure.

And sometimes, I wonder if I'll ever be Impressive and Classic and Chinese enough to be in Auntie Eva's new family.

All these worries bubbled up inside me.

But Auntie Eva was so happy.

And so excited for her Big Day.

Which was hers, not mine.

So just as she finished my braid, I leaned back against her and put my head on her shoulder and said, "Ngoh oi neih." Which is Chinese for "I love you." Just like my Nai Nai had taught me.

"Ngoh oi neih," she said, putting her arm around me and leaning her head against mine.

And, at least just then, that seemed to be enough.

11

THE WHEELS ON THE BUS DRIVE TO BURGER PLANET

My mom says Gwendolyn is such a little person now.

Which is weird.

But also true.

When Gwendolyn was born, she was so small that I could carry her with one arm. (Or I could have, if I'd been allowed to. My parents had A LOT of rules about how I could hold babies, and they all involved two hands.)

But now, Gwendolyn is SO MUCH bigger. She can sit up on her own and crawl (she's *very* fast, and my dad calls her a "speed demon"). And she can even walk, if you hold her hands to keep her up. She eats fruit and small pieces of cheese and likes to hold her own spoon. And she LOVES her hair, and every morning I help her brush it, which makes her laugh and say "Rara!"

So I'll say, "Yes, Gwendolyn—hair! But what are *you*?"

She still hasn't given me an answer, but we're working on it.

Gwendolyn's learning lots of new words too, though NONE of them are "Cilla." Words like "uh-oh." And "gwoth" (gross). And, worst of all, "no."

Which is a word that Gwendolyn says A LOT.

For example, when we had a family dinner at Grandma and Grandpa Jenkins's house last week, a few days before we left for Auntie Eva's wedding, "no" was pretty much the only thing Gwendolyn said. She didn't want to sit in her high chair, she didn't want to drink from her new sippy cup, and when my dad handed her a spoon, she yelled, "No!" and threw it, which scared Daisy and made her jump off Nai Nai's lap to hide behind my legs.

Then Gwendolyn didn't want to sit with anyone but my mom, not even when my dad, Nai Nai, or Grandma Jenkins tried to take her. Then I tried to take her because I know all the songs she likes, but when I sat down with her, she squirmed and pushed against me and said, "NO! Mama!"

Which wasn't very nice.

Grandma Jenkins says it's just a phase, and my dad said, "Well, she's stubborn, just like her mother."

Then Ye Ye said, "Well, I don't know, I remember a certain four-year-old who drew on the white couch with permanent marker and then tried to blame it on his little sister. Who was just a few weeks old at the time."

And then my dad didn't know what to say and got quiet, and my mom said, "What?! Tell me *everything*!"

Ye Ye and I giggled, and then there were some GREAT stories. So I guess that made up for it.

At dinner we talked about all of our trips,

because we're all getting to the wedding in different ways. Nai Nai and Ye Ye are driving down early to help Auntie Eva get ready. Grandma and Grandpa Jenkins are taking a plane to the wedding, which is exciting because Grandpa Jenkins promised to bring me a bag of peanuts from the airplane. And we're driving too, just before the wedding.

Everyone was excited, though I wish Nai Nai or Ye Ye or my dad had said more about the wedding to prepare Grandma Jenkins. Because I think she's expecting a Traditional Jenkins wedding, with hats and lots of forks in the right places and fewer chopsticks.

But when I said, "Ye Ye, tell Grandma Jenkins about the tea," he just said, "Oh, yes, there will be a tea ceremony," and Grandma Jenkins said, "Lovely." So now I worry that she's expecting fancy tea and saucers and little sandwiches on plates, so I think I actually made things worse, not better.

But at least we all had a good time.

And Daisy most of all, because now I, Grandpa Jenkins, *and* Nai Nai try to sneakily feed her scraps under the table.

Now we're in the car again, on the way to Auntie Eva's wedding. Leaving for the trip was kind of sad because I had to say goodbye to Colleen, and we won't see each other for THREE WEEKS, because she's going away to a soccer camp just before I get back. But she says she'll send me letters while she's gone, and I've promised to save her a petal from my basket, so at least we have some things to look forward to.

The fact that Gwendolyn says "no" to everything now means that there's not *quite* as much "Wheels on the Bus" this trip (though it's still her favorite, and she still says "buh!" A LOT). And I have to admit that her talking is making the car ride more fun. So far, I've taught her "tu-new!" (tunnel), "caw" (car), and "Bgah-Pan!" (Burger

Planet). (Though you'll notice that all these words have a common Theme, which is that NONE of them is even CLOSE to Cilla.)

But she's learning quickly. And I taught her to say "Burger Planet" because there are Burger Planets EVERYWHERE and Gwendolyn LOVES them. Which goes to show that she has good taste in (some of) the words she uses.

Burger Planets have been an EXCELLENT Theme during this trip, even though my mom keeps saying, "I swear, if I never see another Burger Planet again, it will be too soon." But I think we keep going there so Gwendolyn and I can run around in the playspace. Plus it's the best, so that helps.

We stopped at a Burger Planet yesterday, actually. And after we ate, we went to the playground and I made a new friend.

At first I was going to play by myself.

But then my dad took Gwendolyn to the little kid area, and I found myself looking at the kids in the ball pit, and it looked really fun.

"Do you want me to walk over with you?" my mom asked.

"Yes, please," I said, and I took her hand.

Just as we walked up, I saw a girl standing by the entrance to the ball pit, about my age, with her mom and dad behind her.

She saw me. I smiled. And then she smiled.

So I didn't even need my mom to come with me after all. I went up to her, all by myself, and asked her to play.

My new friend's name was Emily Fong. She was very nice, and she really liked playing Lava Rescue in the ball pit. And our parents got along and even sat together.

Emily doesn't have a younger sister or brother and really wanted to play with Gwendolyn. So after a while, we went to sit with her in the toddler area, and my dad went to talk with her parents close by.

We were playing a block game and making our blocks spin very fast for Gwendolyn when a man who was standing nearby with his own kids came over to us.

"Wow, what great sisters," he said, motioning to us all.

"Um," I said. Emily and I looked at each other uncertainly.

"Not really," I said.

"Yeah." Emily nodded. "It's like I don't even know her."

"Ooookay." The man laughed uncertainly.

My dad walked over to see what was going on.

"Oh, hi," the man said. "I was just saying what a beautiful family you have. How far apart are they?"

"No idea," my dad answered, honestly.

"Oooookay," the man said again, now really confused. And then he walked away as Emily and I started to giggle. My dad smiled at us, shook his head, and walked back to sit with the grown-ups.

"You were really funny," I said to Emily.

"Well, so were you," she said.

"It's so weird how that happens." I sighed.

"Yeah." Emily sighed. "Tell me about it."

"*Yah!*" Gwendolyn sighed and shook her head just like us, because she clearly wanted to play too.

So we laughed and went to play with the spinning blocks again.

And the more we played, the stranger it all seemed, because we clearly weren't all sisters, I thought, as we ran around the toddler play area. First off, we didn't look alike at all, other than the fact that both of our dads are Chinese and our moms aren't. But there were lots of things that were really different about us, like Emily's freckles and green eyes and curly light brown hair. (Gwendolyn and I have none of these things, which is too bad because I LOVE the word "freckle" and think they'd be exciting to have.)

But it was more than that, too. Emily doesn't spend that much time with little kids. So when Gwendolyn started to Fuss, she thought something was wrong and didn't understand that she was just bored and we needed to distract her with a different game. And when Emily played peekaboo with Gwendolyn, she didn't understand that you have to wait and create just the right amount of

Suspense, long enough to make Gwendolyn giggle, short enough that she doesn't forget you're there. And Emily didn't know that we had to watch Gwendolyn every second, because she crawls *very* fast, and she was REALLY impressed when I caught Gwendolyn every time she tried to speed-crawl to the big kids' area.

And if that man had just been looking, and actually seeing us, he would have known right away who the actual sisters were.

So it was nice, after we'd said goodbye to Emily (which was sad, and I wish we lived closer together), when my dad said, "Gwendolyn was having the best time with you today. We could hear her laughing from across the play space."

"Thanks," I said with a smile as I climbed into my seat.

"Well, thank *you*," he said as he finished buckling Gwendolyn in. "You're a great big sister."

The car started again, and I listened to its humming sounds. I thought about my dad and Auntie Eva, and how she always asks my dad for advice, and how they always make sure to visit each other on birthdays and call when they know the other is upset. And I wondered if that would happen when I was older and Gwendolyn could talk and (finally) say my name.

I wondered what she'll be like, and what I'll be like. And if people will be able to see that we're sisters. I wondered if I'll know the right things to say to her, and the right advice to give her, and if I'll be able to take care of her when she's grown-up and her own person.

And I would have thought about all of this some more, but just then, Batman flew into my lap.

"Buh!" Gwendolyn said from her car seat, looking at me with a hopeful smile. "Buh!"

So I smiled, and my dad laughed, and my mom sighed.

And at least just then, I knew *exactly* what to do.

THE UNEXPECTED

A rehearsal dinner is (yet) another wedding Tradition. It's all about making sure that everything goes just how you imagined it (which is another way of saying perfectly). So as you can maybe guess, I approve of this and wish we could have rehearsals for more things in life, like maybe relay races, and math tests, and making new friends, because then everything would be just like it should be all the time.

Which would be nice.

On the night of the rehearsal dinner, I wore a purple dress that my mom had helped me choose, and Gwendolyn wore a bright pink dress with yellow polka dots and matching barrettes. My mom let me brush Gwendolyn's hair and put it in pigtails, and she giggled and said "Rara!" and then "Bah-man!" So I made sure she had him with her to keep her company at dinner.

While I got ready, I practiced one of the Chinese sentences my Nai Nai had taught

me, saying it over and over in my head. I must have looked nervous, because my mom asked if I wanted to practice my flower girl walk. And when I did, she clapped and said, "Perfect! See, sweetheart? Nothing to worry about."

But she was wrong.

We drove up to a big, beautiful brick building. When we walked in the front door, I saw Nai Nai in her blue dress and Ye Ye in a white shirt and the red-striped tie I'd helped him pick. And then I turned around and saw—

"Auntie Eva!" I went running.

"Cilla!" She picked me up and spun me around (like always). She looked BEAUTIFUL in a white dress that wasn't her wedding one (or at least I hoped not). Because even though it was pretty, it was short and not glittery, and there was no lace anywhere.

Then Auntie Eva put me down and turned to a smiling man in a blue shirt who'd just walked up next to her.

"Cilla," Auntie Eva said, "this is Paul."

Paul was tall with black hair and smiling, crinkly eyes. He seemed very nice.

"Hello," I said, and my voice had gone a bit whispery. I tried to smile but I couldn't quite. Because I knew this was it.

My chance.

The moment I'd imagined so perfectly.

I took a deep breath and stood very straight and remembered the words my Nai Nai had taught me, and the few extra ones I'd asked Melvin to help me with.

"GU JEUNG, NEI HO MAH! NGOH HO GO HING GIEN DOE NEI!" I said perfectly, just like I'd been taught. (Well, maybe a little louder than I'd been taught.) This means, "Hello, Uncle! I'm very happy to meet you!" Or, "HELLO, UNCLE! I'M VERY HAPPY TO MEET YOU!" if you want to get technical. I held my breath.

Paul blinked.

I blinked.

He smiled, a bit uncertainly.

I smiled, a bit uncertainly.

And I felt my heart pounding and a nervous feeling in my stomach. Had I said it wrong? Was my accent bad? Had I ruined my chance to be in Auntie Eva's new family the very first time I met her new husband?

"Um . . . ," Paul said, looking down at me and then sideways at Auntie Eva, who had her hand over her mouth and a funny expression on her face. "So . . . ," he said.

My heart raced.

"So . . . I'm Korean," he said finally.

"WHAT?" I said.

And Auntie Eva started to *laugh*.

"I'm sorry, I thought you knew that," she said, bending down to put her hands on my shoulders. "Paul doesn't speak any Chinese. But that was *so* sweet of you!"

She gave me a BIG hug.

And then, as I stood there too stunned to move, she told Paul what I had said.

"I'm so happy to meet you too, Cilla." Paul smiled down at me. "Eva's told me all about you. And your

Chinese sounded *much* better than mine. I learned a few sentences so I could greet your Nai Nai and Ye Ye, and your E-Pah and E-Gung. But," he said, leaning in like it was a secret, "I TOTALLY messed things up. They were all nice about it, so I think I

made an okay impression. But don't tell anyone," he said, making a funny, scared kind of face.

Then I giggled, and he and Auntie Eva laughed. He held out his hand, and I shook it. Just like a grown-up would.

The rest of the night went pretty much as expected. Nai Nai loved my surprise when Auntie Eva told her about it and said my Chinese had been *perfect*. And during the rehearsal, someone told me just where to stand and when to walk. I walked slowly and in a straight line, just like my mom and dad had shown me. And my Nai Nai and Ye Ye hummed a wedding song when they practiced walking Auntie Eva down the aisle, and it made her sniffle, but in a nice way.

Later, at the rehearsal dinner, Auntie Eva introduced me to Paul's mom and dad, Mr. and Mrs. Kim. They seemed nice, and I tried to remember all my manners and shook their hands too. And it was actually a relief not to worry about

Traditions and if they'd be upset if I didn't know them all. Though they were very quiet, and Mrs. Kim had a stern face and I wondered if that was how she always looked or if she was just Not Happy right now. And I noticed that she and Mr. Kim were sitting by Nai Nai and Ye Ye, but they didn't seem to have much to talk about. Which was strange, because Ye Ye tells the *best* stories, so dinner with him always has talking and laughing.

I got distracted, though, and stopped watching Nai Nai and Ye Ye's table because I was busy playing with Paul's cousin Noah, the boy I'd seen in the picture who I'd thought was Paul's brother. (Technically, Noah told me, he's Paul's second cousin. I thought this meant he was Paul's second cousin ever, but then my mom explained that it means one of his parents is Paul's cousin. So that was another expression I'd had no idea about, and I wonder why people can't actually just say what they mean.)

Anyway, Noah's younger than I am and will be carrying the rings, just like Alien-Face McGee did.

"You're different than I'd thought you'd be," I

told him while we waited for dinner. "Auntie Eva showed us a fancy picture of you all, sitting in a restaurant."

Noah rolled his eyes.

"Oh, that was for my harabeoji's birthday party. That's 'grandpa' in Korean. We were at his favorite Korean restaurant, and my mom made me put gel in my hair and everything, and it was SO GROSS. And I spilled tea on myself right afterward, so it really wasn't worth all the ironing and getting new fancy clothes."

I giggled because I knew *exactly* what that felt like.

Noah was fun to play with, and when he didn't know what the foods were at the rehearsal dinner (it *was* a Chinese banquet, like my dad had said it would be), I explained them to him and recommended all my favorites. And then he kept saying things like "Wait until you see the Korean outfits they wear tomorrow" and "Wait until you meet my Auntie Jenny and Uncle Mike" and "You're going to love my cousin Sammy. He'll be there tomorrow too, and you two will definitely be friends!"

Noah was impressed by the banquet, especially when he realized there would be more than six courses, and he LOVED the roast duck, lobster, abalone, and noodles. Though not the jellyfish, which is fair, because they're kind of funny-looking and you really have to get used to the taste. Not to mention the texture.

There was more food than I've ever seen in my life at that banquet, and I agreed with Grandpa Jenkins when he leaned back happily in his chair and said, "I don't know if I'll ever be hungry again."

But when the desserts came out, Grandpa Jenkins and I changed our minds *very* fast. Because after the Traditional Chinese banquet, we had Traditional Korean desserts. There were plates piled high with beautiful purple and pink and white cakes that Noah explained were made of sweet rice called *tteok* and then filled with red bean paste (and you know how I feel about red bean paste).

So I was very full and happy when I got into my couch bed this evening. My mom kissed me on the forehead and said, "Sleep well, sweetheart. Tomorrow's going to be so much fun."

I smiled, and thought about how Auntie Eva

looked so happy, and how much I really liked Paul, and how nice the idea of having Noah in my family is.

And I realized how excited I am for the wedding.

Now I'm writing on my hotel couch bed.

And I'm thinking about what I've learned and how many surprises I've had.

There's still a part of me that worries, because I hope Nai Nai and Ye Ye and Mr. Kim and Mrs. Kim can Get Along and be friends.

Because I know how these things can be. It took a long time for my family to start being a family, all together. And the Lees and the Kims seem really, really different.

But I'm also thinking about Paul learning Chinese words. And how Auntie Eva's wearing a Traditional Korean dress tomorrow.

Which makes me feel better.

So I'm going to go to sleep, because tomorrow is THE Big Day, and I want to be ready.

And I've decided that I'm not going to be nervous anymore about tomorrow. Because now all I have to do is be a good flower girl and do everything just like I did in the rehearsal. And I know I can do that.

I'm a future author extraordinaire, and a future Classic author, after all.

And besides, all the unexpected has already happened.

What could possibly go wrong?

THE BIG DAY

The morning of the wedding was busier than I'd thought it would be. Of course, I know by now that weddings take a lot of preparation, but we'd already done SO much and what could there *possibly* be left to do?!

But when I said this to my mom, she just laughed.

And now, I'll admit that I can understand why.

Because the answer to this question is: A LOT.

First, everyone had to take a shower, and there was a lot of scrubbing and cleaning. My mom put special gel in my hair and used a *hair dryer*, which was a Big Deal because this is something I only get to do for VERY special occasions. And as she did my hair, I sat very still and reminded myself that I'd decided not to be nervous.

I did a pretty good job of this too. In fact, while my mom was doing the finishing touches with the curling iron (which I've never been allowed to use before), she paused and said, "You haven't said a word all morning, Cilla. You okay?"

"Yes," I said, keeping as still as possible. "I'm just being calm. And grown-up."

My mom put a hand on my face and looked at me in the mirror.

"You're already *so* grown-up, my special girl," she said. "All you need to do today is have fun." Then, "Tell you what—when we get to the ceremony hall, I promise that one of us will be there to keep you company and to help you not be nervous, until right before the ceremony. Okay?"

And finally, I smiled. Because I liked this plan.

After lunch, we took my dress from the closet, and my mom walked me down the hallway to the

big room where my Auntie Eva and all her brides-
maids were getting ready.

Jane opened the door for us, and I know my
eyes got big, because there were people *everywhere*, all not ready yet, with curlers in their hair
and silky pink bathrobes, and they were running
around and saying things like, "Linda, have you
seen my lipstick?!"

And at the center of them all, Auntie Eva was
sitting at a table, and someone was brushing light,
just-sparkly-enough powder on her eyes. Her hair
was up in a bun with one curl at the side, and she
looked BEAUTIFUL.

Auntie Eva gave me a big hug (or as much as she
could, because the person doing her makeup said,
"Careful!").

My mom gave me a kiss and left to get ready,
and Jane painted my nails light pink and used the
hair dryer again to help them dry. Then Karen,
who was also really nice, helped me put on what
she said was "just a touch" of makeup, which is a

REALLY grown-up thing, so that was also very exciting.

Nai Nai came in, wearing her glittery purple dress, soon after that, and then Mrs. Kim in a pretty blue one. They gave hugs and said how nice everyone looked, and then they sat together on a couch in the room, though I noticed that they weren't talking very much. And when they did, it was to say things like "Beautiful dress," and "Nice weather," and "What a day," which aren't really that exciting.

So I went over and said hello and asked them if I should have a ribbon in my hair.

They both said yes, which was great, because I know from experience that the more two sides of a family have in common, the better.

And let's be honest—everyone likes ribbons.

After all the hair brushing and spraying and twisting was done, it was (FINALLY!) time for the dresses.

Nai Nai helped me get mine on, and it was soft

and beautiful, and Auntie Eva and all the brides-maids said, "Awww."

Next came the bridesmaids. They put on bright blue dresses and came twirling into the room. Jane did a funny dance, and everyone was having a great and silly time.

Finally, it was Auntie Eva's turn.

When Auntie Eva came out in her dress, which Jane and Nai Nai had helped her put on in the GIANT bathroom, I *gasped*. Because Auntie Eva looked just like a princess, with a poofy dress, no sparkles (sadly), but LOTS of lace that shimmered and made swishing sounds when she moved.

There was nothing to do but clap. And though Nai Nai tried to hide it, we all saw her sniffle when Jane helped Auntie Eva put on her long white veil, which clipped into her hair and swirled down the back of her dress like a shimmery wave. (Which is an *excellent* Simile, if I do say so myself, because this veil only deserves the best. It was that beautiful.)

We went outside to take pictures, and the rest

of our family came to join us. I stood with my mom and dad in some and with Jane and the brides-maids in others. It was fun, though every once in a while I remembered how soon the ceremony was and got a flutter in my stomach. And the photog-rapher said "Smile" so much that sometimes my smile felt watery and not quite real, and it was hard to do it every time she asked. But I tried because I wanted to do everything I could for Auntie Eva's Big Day.

I rode in a LIMO, with Auntie Eva, Nai Nai, Mrs. Kim, and the bridesmaids, and we arrived at the ceremony hall before everyone else did. I was glad, because there weren't lots of people to stare or to make me nervous. But from the room we waited in (which had comfortable couches and platters with pieces of fruit on little sticks), I could hear as people began to arrive. There were A LOT of voices all of a sudden, and I remembered how big the hall had seemed the day before and how many chairs there were. So I tried to take deep breaths, but that didn't quite work because I think the room was dusty and I kept sneezing. And it's hard to look like a responsible flower girl when that happens.

Between my sneezes, I watched my Nai Nai and Mrs. Kim sit quietly by each other. Every few minutes they'd say something, and Auntie Eva started coming over to ask them questions and to say hello. Jane noticed this too, and she came over and sat between them and started asking all about Auntie Eva and Paul when they were younger. Then she started telling jokes, and I wanted to help, so between the sneezing I tried to laugh really hard (though that can be difficult when you're sneezy and nervous). But I think Jane appreciated it.

It seemed to be working a little, though Mrs. Kim was still very quiet and so was Nai Nai, which was frustrating because Nai Nai usually loves jokes (she laughs at all of Ye Ye's even though some of them are definitely more silly than funny). And I wondered why everything had to be so complicated when it comes to families.

I sat there thinking and, I'll admit, worrying.

So it was a big relief when there was a knock on the door and I heard a familiar, jokey voice say, "Hey, sis, what's the occasion?"

"Daddy!" I yelled, running over to him, and he gave me a hug. My mom and Gwendolyn were just outside in the hallway and wanted to see how I was and to keep me company just like they'd promised. My mom wore her beautiful dress with its big skirt, and my dad wore a *suit*, which was fun to see. And Gwendolyn looked excellent in her lacy white-and-light-pink dress, with a pink bow on her head that she kept trying to tug off.

We went into the hallway, and my mom suggested that maybe I could practice there if that would make me feel better. So I started walking up and down the small hallway very slowly, pretending to throw petals from my basket, though it was hard because every once in a while I'd sneeze again. Which was distracting.

Nai Nai came out to talk with my mom and

dad. And a few minutes later, Mrs. Kim came out to say hello to some of Paul's cousins, who had arrived late.

Every time I passed my mom, I squeezed her hand, and it made me feel better. But after a few minutes, someone came up to Mrs. Kim because they were confused about who was handing out programs, so my mom gave Gwendolyn to my dad and went to help. Right after that, there was a question about seats, and my dad gave Gwendolyn to Nai Nai, and he went to go help move things. Suddenly it was just me, Nai Nai, Mrs. Kim, and Gwendolyn in the hallway.

I held my basket very tightly, and tried not to sneeze again, and told myself to just keep walking, up and down.

Suddenly, I heard a familiar voice.

"Cilla, you look *marvelous*," Grandma Jenkins said as she walked over in her special-day hat, the front weighed down by the new white-and-green flower (it was enormous and AMAZING and

Grandma Jenkins was right, because you could barely tell it was plastic).

And I smiled at Grandma Jenkins.

But as I saw her introduce herself to Mrs. Kim, I realized that no one else was wearing a hat. My smile faded, and I wondered what Mrs. Kim thought about Grandma Jenkins.

Especially with that GIANT flower.

"Ellen's still helping with the programs, Rachel," Grandma said, "but I can take Gwendolyn for you, if you need to get ready."

"Thank you," Nai Nai said, and she tried to hand Gwendolyn over to her, but it was hard because Gwendolyn was squirming and making unhappy noises all of a sudden.

And my Grandma's hat was falling over her eyes because of the heavy flower, and Nai Nai was trying to get Gwendolyn to let go of her hair so she wouldn't mess it up, and then *I* started sneezing again and I *couldn't stop.*

And Gwendolyn was saying, "NO!"

And Nai Nai was saying, "Ay yah!"

And Grandma Jenkins was saying, "Oh my goodness gracious!"

And I was saying, "Ah-CHOO!"

So I don't think *anyone* in my family was making a Good Impression AT ALL.

Nai Nai managed to untangle her hair from Gwendolyn's fist, and Grandma Jenkins took her, bouncing her up and down and making soothing noises. But it was loud in the hall, which I know Gwendolyn doesn't like. And then Nai Nai rummaged through the diaper bag my mom had left in the hallway and found Batman, because he usually calms Gwendolyn down.

But when Nai Nai tried to give it to her, Gwendolyn turned her face away. Suddenly her cheeks started turning red, and she scrunched up her face.

And Gwendolyn started to cry. *Loudly.*

"No!" she said, twisting herself around in Grandma Jenkins's arms. "No Bah-man. Rara!"

"Leave your hair alone, Gwendolyn," Grandma

said, bouncing her and trying to check if her diaper was wet. But she couldn't quite get there because her hat started sliding forward again.

"Ay yah!" Nai Nai said, and went to go help, but her arm caught on Grandma Jenkins's purse, and then they had to untangle themselves as Gwendolyn began to *yell*.

"NO," Gwendolyn cried. "Rara!"

I saw my grandmas and my sister tangled up and shushing and yelling.

I know what I have to do, I told myself. *Just keep walking.*

"Gwendolyn, darling, it's okay," Grandma Jenkins said from behind me, and I started my flower girl walk again, up and down.

"Rara!" Gwendolyn's cheeks were red, and her mouth shook.

"Shhhhh," Nai Nai said, in her most calming voice.

"Rara!" Gwendolyn's face was wet with tears.

Mrs. Kim took a step backward.

I kept walking.

"Rara," Gwendolyn sobbed.

No one was helping, and everyone was making a bad impression, and no one was there just for *me*, like my mom had said they would be—

"Rara!"

Now Gwendolyn was having a tantrum, and I was trying to do all these things for her and help her find her Destiny and she never noticed, and she wouldn't say my name, and why should I—

"RARA!" Gwendolyn wailed, in a voice that was sad and, I realized all of a sudden, *scared*.

"Gwendolyn!" I said. And then I was running to her, and she had her arms out to me, and she held me tight, and my Nai Nai caught my basket just before it fell.

"Awww," Mrs. Kim said. She smiled a big smile that made her look soft and friendly and just like Paul. "Of course!" she went on. "She wanted her sister. I should have known."

And Grandma and Nai Nai at the same time said, "Oh!"

I looked at them, because I didn't understand.

And then I looked down at Gwendolyn. Who
looked up at me, and sniffled, and said "Rara"
again. This time happily.

"You . . . ," I said, feeling my breath come in a
little gasp, finally understanding. "You've been
saying my name, Gwendolyn. You've been saying it
this whole time."

"Rara," she said, looking up at me.

As if it was the most obvious thing in the world.

And then there was nothing to do but hold on
to her, as she held on to me, tightly.

In a few minutes, Gwendolyn was calm. I wiped
her cheeks with the edge of my sleeve, and it was
like she'd never been upset in the first place.

"It's almost time," Grandma Jenkins said quietly. "I should take her back now, so you can get
ready." Gwendolyn Fussed when I let go, but she
didn't cry.

Nai Nai handed me my basket of petals again. I sneezed.

"Ay yah," she said.

"I think you're allergic," Mrs. Kim said.

"I can hold them far away from my face," I suggested. But I sneezed again right after that, and I wasn't so sure.

"Hmmmm . . ." Mrs. Kim looked at me with a frown, and I tried to smile but I was scared because maybe I was going to ruin Auntie Eva's wedding after all, because who's ever heard of a flower girl with no flowers?

"I have an idea," Mrs. Kim said. She smiled and wiggled her eyebrows at me in a way that made me giggle.

Then she told my Grandma and Nai Nai her plan.

"Wonderful," Grandma Jenkins said. "I have just the thing."

"I have a pin," Nai Nai said.

When they were done, they all looked at me, grinning.

"Well." Grandma Jenkins sighed happily. "I

think we make an excellent team, if I do say so myself."

And Nai Nai and Mrs. Kim nodded, looking very pleased with themselves.

"What do you think, Cilla?" Mrs. Kim asked.

And for once, I knew I was right, and not being unrealistic at *all*, when I smiled and said, "It's perfect."

CLASSIC LEE, CLASSIC JENKINS

Traditionally, flower girls walk down the aisle very slowly and carefully, in time with the music, just like I did. Everyone turned to look at me, which is also a wedding Tradition, and even though it was intimidating, it was also nice, because they were all friendly. I could see Grandma and Grandpa Jenkins and my mom and my dad. Paul was standing at the front of the room, and he smiled a big smile at me, so I smiled a big one back.

But in my arms, instead of the Traditional basket or bouquet, or even just one single flower, I carried something else.

Because Traditions are great. So, sometimes, you follow them.

But sometimes, you make your own.

And when I walked down the aisle at Auntie Eva's wedding, I, Cilla Lee-Jenkins, flower girl and future author extraordinaire, carried my little sister, Gwendolyn Lee-Jenkins, Destiny unknown but great, with my Grandma Jenkins's Giant Flower pinned right to the middle of her special white-and-light-pink dress.

Gwendolyn looked around with wide eyes, and every once in a while she chewed (but gently) on the green and white flower petals. But she was very quiet and happy and didn't Fuss at all.

It turns out that most people cry at the "I do's," including my dad, Grandma, Grandpa, Nai Nai, and Ye Ye. And Mr. and Mrs. Kim. And me too, I learned. But not Gwendolyn (which is funny, because she cries at EVERYTHING else, as you probably know by now).

Through it all, Auntie Eva and Paul looked really, really, really happy.

When the wedding was over, we went out into the front big room, where there were snacks. Guests walked around and talked, and my mom and dad gave me big hugs and said, "I'm SO proud of you!"

When Auntie Eva and (I guess now *Uncle*) Paul came out again, they'd changed into what Mrs. Kim explained were Traditional Korean clothes called *hanbok.* She said that there were lots of Traditions about clothes and colors at Korean weddings.

"Just like Chinese weddings!" I said.

"Exactly." She smiled. "That's why I'm wearing blue—it's a Tradition for the mother of the groom."

"Oh!" I said. And this conversation was amazing, and I wanted to know more, but just then, Auntie Eva came swishing over. She looked beautiful in her hanbok. It had lots of bright, bright colors and a HUGE skirt that poofed out and a small pink jacket that I *really* want. And Paul followed behind her wearing a colorful shirt and a vest and baggy, silky bright pants.

"Time for the ceremony," Auntie Eva said, taking my hand in one hand and Mrs. Kim's in the other.

"You're going to love this one, Cilla," Paul said with a smile, and I gave him a big smile back.

We went into another room, which had been set up with a table on the floor. Noah explained that this was part of a Traditional Korean ceremony called *pyebaek.* Then Mr. and Mrs. Kim, and Nai

Nai and Ye Ye, and Auntie Eva and Paul sat at the table, and there was lots of bowing, and Nai Nai and Ye Ye did a GREAT job. Then, as if the beautiful clothes weren't enough, after they were done there was another Tradition where Mr. and Mrs. Kim and Nai Nai and Ye Ye threw chestnuts, and Auntie Eva and Paul tried to catch them in a piece of cloth, and it was maybe the BEST Tradition I HAVE EVER SEEN (other than Chinese New Year, of course). And Grandma Jenkins said, "What fun!" even though I know she *definitely* doesn't think that throwing things is Proper. Then Paul gave Auntie Eva a piggyback ride, which was nice of him.

As Noah and I cheered and Gwendolyn yelled happily and clapped her hands, I realized that Traditions can be great, even when you don't know every single thing about them.

In fact, it was nice to just enjoy them.

"So," I asked my Nai Nai, as the ceremony ended and we walked behind Auntie Eva back into the front room, "will they have Korean and Chinese Traditions in their family all the time?"

"Yes," Nai Nai said. "And when they have children, your cousins will be Chinese-Korean-American."

"Mom!" Auntie Eva sighed. But her sigh was in a laughing, happy kind of way. "I just got married," she said. "Give us some time."

"I just thought she'd like to know," Nai Nai said with a little smile.

"I knew this would happen," Auntie Eva said to me, grinning. "Your parents warned me. You get married, and people keep looking for that gleam in your eye."

"Stomachs," I corrected her (but nicely). "Babies grow in stomachs, not eyes."

Auntie Eva and Nai Nai both laughed then.

"It's an expression, sweetie," Auntie Eva said. "About babies."

And I'm not ashamed to admit that that's one I did NOT get.

Auntie Eva and Uncle Paul changed back into their wedding ceremony clothes, and we all went back into the big main room. All the chairs had been cleared away, and there were tables, which was exciting because that meant it was dinnertime.

I sat at a table with my mom and dad, Grandma and Grandpa, and some of my dad and Auntie Eva's friends. Nai Nai and Ye Ye were close by and had me come over to their table, where all my uncles and aunties from Chinatown told me how great a job I'd done.

But that wasn't even the nicest thing anyone said about my being a flower girl. Because as I was walking between tables (wedding dinners go on for a long time, apparently), Jane called me over.

"You did such a good job as the flower girl, Cilla! You and Gwendolyn make a wonderful team." She gave me a hug.

"Thank you," I said. "You were a great maid of honor."

"Thanks. You know," she said, leaning in, "Lucy and I have been talking. Do you think you two would like to be flower girls again, at our wedding?"

"Really?" I gasped (because this is a BIG deal).

"Really."

"Wow," I said. "I do."

"Wonderful!" Jane clapped her hands. "I already spoke to your mom about it, and I'm sure we can get everything arranged. Let's keep it a secret for tonight, though, since it's Eva's Big Day."

"Yes." I smiled. "I understand."

After dinner, we had the tea ceremony. Auntie Eva came out in her red-and-gold cheongsam, and Paul wore a Traditional Chinese outfit that I'd never seen before. It was also silk, with a high neck and pretty patterns. He and Auntie Eva poured tea for Nai Nai and Ye Ye and Mr. and Mrs. Kim and E-Pah and E-Gung and Paul's aunts and uncles. In return, they got little red envelopes with money inside, just like during Chinese New Year. And Mr. and Mrs. Kim did a GREAT job with knowing when to bow. And the whole time, I explained the ceremony to Noah, so he'd know what was going on.

Auntie Eva came over to take a picture with us in her cheongsam, and my dad said, "I'm so happy for you, sis."

"Aw, thanks, big brother," Auntie Eva said, leaning into him and putting her arm around his shoulder. "I'd be lost without you." So then there was even MORE sniffling. (These people.)

Luckily, I was there to make them laugh, because Noah and I showed them a game we'd just made up, which had Tea Ceremony bowing but also involved pyebaek chestnut throwing (we didn't have real chestnuts, but we used our napkins), and the person who caught the most chestnuts would win.

Auntie Eva and Paul went to change (AGAIN), and they came back in the clothes they'd gotten married in (the white poofy dress!) to cut the cake. (Because, as I've mentioned all Traditions come back to cake.) And it was a GIANT cake, with flowers made of frosting and three towering layers, and Auntie Eva made sure I got a piece with a blue flower.

During cake there were speeches, and slide-shows of silly pictures from when Auntie Eva and Paul were kids. And Paul's grandpa sang a song about how happy he was in Korean, and then in English, and then in *Chinese*, and everyone sang along (when they could). Then Jane and Karen, Auntie Eva's two best friends, gave speeches. And they made a great team too.

Then there was something called the Bouquet Toss, and all the bridesmaids and lots of people gathered behind Auntie Eva, and Lucy (who had her hair in a big circle around her head, and it had *flowers in it*) caught the bouquet. Everyone cheered, and Jane *winked* at me, and I winked back.

There were lots and lots of people I didn't know at Auntie Eva and Paul's wedding. But I didn't feel shy, which was funny. And Gwendolyn didn't mind all the people either. Maybe it was because everyone was smiling and because people kept coming over to us and saying things like, "I'm Paul's aunt, welcome to the family!" or "We're so happy Paul met Eva!"

And when people weren't coming over and

saying hello, or when I wasn't talking with my mom or dad or anyone else at my table, I was happy to sit quietly and just look around and see everyone laughing and having such a nice time.

It was during one of these quiet moments that I saw Auntie Eva singing something to Paul. I saw him laughing and clapping, and it looked like he was really enjoying whatever it was. I made a note to ask.

But I didn't have to.

Because just before the final toasting, Auntie Eva came by to take a family photo.

It took a while to organize, because Nai Nai and Ye Ye came to be in the picture with us, but then left to get Grandma and Grandpa Jenkins, because Nai Nai wouldn't take it without them. And as everyone got in a line, Auntie Eva put her arm around Nai Nai's shoulder.

"I'll admit, Mom," she said, "you were right about the photos."

"So you'll always remember your special day," Nai Nai said, putting an arm around her too.

"Thanks for everything, Mom," Auntie Eva said, resting her head on Nai Nai's shoulder. And then she said, "Say cheese!"

And we did.

There was a click and the flash of a camera, and then I saw Paul run over and say, "Sorry—I was talking to my grandpa. I want to be in one!"

My mom bounced Gwendolyn and I got ready to smile again, though I'd been doing it for *so* long that day that my cheeks felt kind of tired.

"Say cheese," Auntie Eva said again.

"Say cake," my dad said.

"Say 'earwax on a stick,'" Paul said.

"You know 'earwax on a stick'?!!!" There was a clicking sound and the flash of a camera light as I turned to him, wide-eyed.

"Your aunt sang it to me," he said. "I LOVE it."

"You remembered it?" I asked, turning to Auntie Eva.

"Of course, silly," she laughed. "How could I forget? It's a family Classic."

"*WOW,*" I said. Then, "Are you *sure?*"

"Positive." Auntie Eva smiled. "It's one for the history books."

I couldn't say anything else for a long, long moment.

Then my mom put her hand on my shoulder and said, "Let's try that again, Cilla."

So I turned to the camera and said, "Cheese," and Gwendolyn said, "Rara!"

The camera flashed, and we stood there—my Auntie Eva, my Uncle Paul, my mom and dad, my Nai Nai and Ye Ye, my Grandma and Grandpa Jenkins, my sister Gwendolyn, and me, Priscilla Lee-Jenkins, Classic Author.

And this time, smiling wasn't hard *at all*.

The tables were cleared away for dancing, and we all stood around the dance floor. Auntie Eva and Paul twirled around for the first dance, while we clapped and my mom cried and my dad made fun of her. But then he got sniffly too. (He can't fool me. I'm a Classic Author, after all.)

I didn't see how the night could get much better after that.

But it turns out, it could.

Because as another song started, Auntie Eva yelled, "Who wants to dance with us?!" And Nai Nai and Grandpa Jenkins were the first to run out, then Grandma Jenkins and Mr. Kim, and Mrs. Kim and Ye Ye. So I clapped and cheered, like everyone else. Gwendolyn did too.

And then it happened.

The music started going faster. And suddenly, Gwendolyn began to move.

First one foot. Then the other.

She shook. She wiggled.

And then, only using my skirt to keep herself up, she stood there, almost all by herself, smiling as she looked up at me.

Dancing.

"Look at that!" my dad said, walking over.

"Hey." My mom came up behind him. "Someone's got rhythm," she said as Gwendolyn swayed and punched an arm in the air.

"Wow!" People were stopping to watch. "Look at her go."

"Gwendolyn," I said as people began to dance around us. "This is *it*! Your Destiny! You're a future dance legend!"

"Rara!" she yelled happily.

And I knew that meant we'd found it.

On the night I became a Classic Author and my little sister found her Destiny, we stayed up waaaaay past our bedtime. My dad danced the silly dances that make my mom giggle, and my mom danced them too. Noah and his cousin Sammy spun each other around in circles, and Paul's grandfather danced around his walker and clicked his heels. Grandma and Grandpa Jenkins showed us something called the jitterbug, and there was lots of kicking and stepping and twirling.

In the center of the room, Auntie Eva and Paul danced and laughed, and Paul showed me some funny dance moves that he likes to call "The Sprinkler," "The Shopping Cart," and "Drinking Spoiled Milk."

Through it all, I held Gwendolyn's hands, so she could dance standing up as all our grandparents, and Mr. and Mrs. Kim, spun around us.

And together, we tore up the dance floor.

EPILOGUE: A CLIFF-HANGER (NO ACTUAL CLIFFS INVOLVED)

So I know I said the story was over. And it almost is.

But I thought it would be more exciting if it ended with a Cliff-Hanger.

A Cliff-Hanger is a Classic way to end a story, because writers use them all the time. It's not about actual cliffs (which is lucky, because I wouldn't want to hang off a cliff, no matter how Classic it was).

In the literary world, though, a Cliff-Hanger is about Suspense and usually has surprise. A Cliff-Hanger doesn't quite tell you everything about an ending, which means you can't wait to know what's going to happen next.

And my book *really* ends in a Cliff-Hanger, because it has A LOT of Suspense and a BIG surprise, and even *I* don't know what's going to happen next.

Auntie Eva and Paul had driven off in a fancy black car with streamers at the back, and we all waved and clapped and cheered (and Nai Nai and Mr. Kim cried again, but still in a happy way).

But just as my mom was turning to my dad and saying, "I guess we should head out soon," Mrs. Kim came up behind her and said, "Who's ready for left-over cake?!"

And I bounced up and down and yelled, "Me!" And so did Grandpa Jenkins, my dad, my mom, and Ye Ye.

We crowded around one of the dinner tables as the last of the guests left, pulling more chairs over because we didn't have enough. The grown-ups sipped from their tall, fancy glasses, and we ate left-over wedding cake with our fingers off of paper napkins. Mrs. Kim and Grandpa Jenkins talked about baseball, and Mr. Kim and my dad were laughing over silly jokes. Noah's mom was telling my mom a story while Noah dozed in her lap, and Ye Ye had just wiped frosting on Nai Nai's nose, which made her say, "Ay yah!" (And then she wiped some on his cheek when he wasn't looking and winked when I saw her do it.)

And everyone was laughing and smiling, and me most of all.

Because even though I'd known that most Traditions involve cake, I hadn't realized that cake is something that ties ALL Traditions together—Kim, Lee, and Jenkins alike.

I was sitting, and eating, and laughing, and helping Gwendolyn get crumbs out of her hair, when it happened.

Mr. Kim said, "One last toast. To our new family!"

And Grandpa Jenkins said, "Hear, hear!"

And Grandma Jenkins picked up the bottle of special bubbly drink and went to refill everyone's fancy glasses.

When, suddenly, EVERYTHING changed.

"Champagne, Ellen?" Grandma asked, turning to my mom.

"No, thanks," Mom said. "I've just been drinking water."

I didn't think this was a big deal.

But my Grandma looked at my mom for a minute, with her head turned a little sideways, just the way my mom does when she's thinking.

Then, slowly, my mom smiled. And suddenly, my Grandma smiled a big smile back.

"I thought you had a certain gleam in your eye!" Grandma Jenkins grinned.

"Uh-oh, Gwendolyn." I turned to her. Gwendolyn looked up at me, a fistful of cake halfway to her mouth, her eyes big.

"We're in trouble now."

GLOSSARY:
CILLA'S TERMS FOR LIFE
AND (CLASSIC) LITERATURE

Ay yah:

This is a Chinese way of saying "Wow!" or "Goodness!" or "Oh no!" or "What?!" or pretty much anything.

Cheongsam:

A BEAUTIFUL Chinese dress. I have one, Auntie Eva has one, Nai Nai has one, Mom has one (which she wore at her own wedding). When Gwendolyn gets bigger, she'll have one too.

Classic:

This is a book that stays around FOREVER. There are lots of different kinds of Classic stories, like

Legends and Adventures and Romances. If you want to write a Classic, I'd suggest putting these Themes in it. And also maybe a dragon or two, because they're the best.

Cliff-Hanger:

When you end a story with suspense (but no actual cliffs are needed).

Drama:

What you use to make things exciting. Pirates help.

Golly:

The Jenkins version of "Ay yah" and "Wah!" (see *Ay yah* and *Wha*)

Hanbok:

BEAUTIFUL Korean clothes. Auntie Eva's was colorful and bright, and between her hanbok and her cheongsam (see *Cheongsam*), I think Auntie Eva probably has the best wardrobe *ever*.

Moon cake:

A Traditional Chinese cake filled with lotus or red bean paste and a salty egg. It's delicious.

Moral:

A lesson you learn after a story. The best have frogs.

Nai Nai:

The Chinese word for "Grandmother." It took a while for my Grandpa Jenkins to figure out that you say this as "Nigh Nigh" not "Nee Nee" or "Nay Nay." And when he finally got it, he said, "Golly!" (see *Golly*)

Precision of Language:

Saying what you mean. This is very helpful for using your words and having people understand you. Also, when your dad says, "Young Lady, you need to behave right now," and you say, "Precision of Language, Daddy. I *am* behaving, I'm just behaving badly," he doesn't know what to say, and the look on his face is funny, though you'll have to go to your room after, so choose your moments carefully.

Pyebaek:

This is a Korean wedding Tradition, and it's AMAZING. It involves beautiful outfits, a lot of bowing, chestnuts, tea drinking, and piggyback rides. I highly recommend it.

Simile:

When you compare two things using the word "like" or "as." So, for example, "Daisy is as dainty as a sea slug. But I love her, plus she's cuddly like a teddy bear."

Tea ceremony:

This is a Chinese wedding Tradition. It also involves beautiful outfits (see *Cheongsam*), bowing, and tea drinking (though sadly there are no piggyback rides).

Theme:

Something that happens over and over again. So, it's a BIG Theme whenever I miss the ball in gym class. But then Colleen says, "Don't worry, Cilla, you did great!" Because Colleen is the best, which is another Theme in my life.

Tradition:

Something you do because that's the way it's been done for a loooong time. There's lots of cake, like moon cakes (see *Moon cake*) and tteok (see *Tteok*), and lots of beautiful dresses (see *Pyebaek* and *Tea ceremony*).

Tteok:

A Traditional Korean cake made of sweet rice. It's also delicious, which is a big Theme with cake (see *Theme*).

Wah:

A Chinese way of saying "Oh!" or "Oh my" or "Huh?" or "Great!" or anything else you feel "Ay yah" isn't getting across.

Ye Ye:

The Chinese word for "Grandfather." You say this

as "Yeh Yeh," not "Yee Yee" or "Yay Yay." Though usually you wouldn't be saying this, because only I call my Ye Ye "Ye Ye." But now Alien-Face McGee does too, and his pronunciation is EXCELLENT.

Young Lady:

Usually what you are when you're in trouble, but recently it's also been a nice thing, like when your mom starts to cry because you're technically a fourth grader and says, "You're such a Young Lady now!" So it's a weird one.

ACKNOWLEDGMENTS

Writing a second book has been a daunting but joyful process, and I am so grateful for all who helped me see it through.

Thank you to Connie Hsu for all you continue to teach me about writing, craft, and stories. Thank you to Amy Lin for your input and expert eye. Thank you to Megan Abbate for everything you do, and for putting up with all manner of questions and concerns. Thank you to Beth Clark for your beautiful book design. And thank you to Mary Van Akin, Tiara Kittrell, Caitlin Sweeney, Lucy Del Priore, Katie Halata, and everyone else at Roaring Brook—I am so grateful that Cilla and I found a home with you!

Thank you to Dana Wulfekotte for your exquisite drawings, which never fail to make me laugh and move me. Your illustrations for this book gave me everything I ever envisioned for Cilla (PLUS Batman in a tutu!).

Thank you to Dan Lazar, agent, advocate, and constant presence in every element of this process. Thank you to Torie for all your help, and for putting up with my perennially late e-mails.

I am so lucky to be supported by amazing communities of writers, scholars, mentors, and friends. Thank you to the Writers' Room of Boston, which gave me a home, and to Debka, Alexander, and Camille. Thank you to all my friends and colleagues at UMass Boston: Cheryl, Renata, Sam, Louise, Hugh, Sarah, Dan, and Matt. Thank you to my ChLA crew, and my community of children's lit scholars—Micki, Dawn, Amy, Ally, Cathie, Sarah, Stacey, Kazia, and Breanna—you are astounding! Thank you to the Mr. Crepe Group: Rachel, Marcy-Kate, Mackenzi, Kip, and so many others! And thank you to the Seventeen Debuts (it's been such a joy getting to know you!). Thank you to Katie Bayerl, Karen McManus, Kate Slivensky, Sarah Horowitz, Greg Katsoulis, and Lisa Rosinsky. Thank you to Karen, Faith, and the Concord Public Library. Thank you to the communities of teachers who continue to teach and inspire me: Ms. Davies, Bob Bell, Tom Kohut, Maria Nikolajeva, Morag Styles, Prifti, and, of course, Mr. Flight. Thank you to Porter Square Books for giving Cilla such a warm welcome into the world. And thank you to Diesel Cafe for housing me as I wrote a good chunk of this book!

Thank you to my friends; I am so grateful to have you all in my life. Thank you, Becky, for being my launch companion, and for the inspiration that your beautiful words and stories always offer. Thank you, Valerie, for our evening chats and ice-cream-delivery housemate parties. Thank you, Kate, for the chocolate, friendship, and golden writing afternoons (I stole your living room for a

setting in this book—I hope you don't mind!).
Thank you, Emily Jaeger—you're a perennial cure
for my shyness, and I'd walk across a crowded
room (or indoor playground) for you any day.
Thank you to friends near and far who have supported me and Cilla from day one: Olivia, Emily
Rockett, Erica, Perri, Zoe, Alice, and Ian. And of
course, thank you, Ashley, Hannah, and Yanie, for
always being there, for unscheduled phone calls that
last for hours, for making distance seem like nothing, and for teaching me that you can never have
too many best friends.

A huge thank-you to Ben, Courtney, Colleen,
and Annalee for once again letting me draw on
shared memories from childhood. Thank you to
Kiyoshi for the Burger King car ride. And the
fondest of thank-yous to Melissa Hernandez, a
true friend.

And thank you, finally, to my family. Thank
you to Nai Nai, Ye Ye, E-Pah, and Dede—you are so
present in all the loving memories of this book.

Thank you, Charles, Henry, Ethan, Martina, Dan, Courtney, and Aysun.

Thank you, Auntie Esther and Uncle Paul. Your influence is all over this book, and not simply in the Chinese phrases you helped me learn as I wrote it. Thank you for your love and encouragement, your enthusiasm and joy, and for teaching me to make dumplings and Hong Kong-style tea.

Kimmy, Yvonne, Jenn, you're all present in this book, as are Jeff, Paul, and Mike. Thank you all for letting me draw on your stories. Thank you, Jenn, for your example and inspiration, for your house, stunning career, beautiful family, and everything in between. Thank you, Mike, for your support and example (the Harry Potter glasses almost made it into this book—next time!!). Thank you, Yvonne, for letting me draw on your wedding and all your (AMAZING) outfit changes. Thank you, Paul, for helping me with Korean Traditions, for letting me draw on your wedding (and your name!!), and for all the incredible dance moves. Thank you,

Kimmy—so many of the tea ceremony details were from your beautiful wedding! Thank you to Jeff for carrying the flower girl (and giant flower!) down the aisle. And thank you to Jeremy for the beautiful Cilla artwork, to Rachel for inspiring me and showing me just how fun frogs can be, to Ellie for being a future dance legend, and to Emmett and Noah. I'll get all your names in a book someday, I promise!

Thank you, Grandmom and Bobby, for the home I always have with you. Thank you, Bobby, for all the roller-skating trips, and thank you, Grandmom, for the afternoons talking about art in your study. And thank you both for humoring my obsession with your dog, Maisy, who's lying on my lap and snoring as I write this.

Thank you to my sisters, Catherine (I'm sorry people call you "The Blob" now) and Sarah (I promise I'll put you in a book too). Thank you, Catherine, for helping me come up with one of my favorite lines in the book, helping me through thorny scenes, and showing me that being a big sister is actually great. Thank you, Sarah, for listening to my book woes, for your help with difficult sections, and, of course, for "Rara!"

Thank you to my dad, Victor, for telling me stories, for teaching me Chinese pronunciation, and for your endless enthusiasm and support.

And finally, thank you to my mom, Julie. Thank you for being there through every up and down, for supporting me at every juncture with love and patience. Thank you for a lifetime of putting up with frogs, "The Wheels on the Bus," and a daughter with a very overactive imagination.

And to my whole family: thank you for the traditions you've taught me, and for the ones we've made.

QUESTIONS FOR THE AUTHOR

SUSAN TAN

What did you want to be when you grew up?
I think it was a ballerina-firefighter author (I aimed high).

If you were a superhero, what would your superpower be?
I'd love to be able to speak and understand every language of the world—does that count?

If you could travel in time, where would you go and what would you do?
I think I'd like to go back and see what life was like for my family several generations ago. Both sides of my family immigrated to the US under pretty hard circumstances, and they had to leave a lot of things behind. In many cases, they didn't want to talk about their old lives—it was too painful, and they wanted to focus on the new ones they were making here. So there's a lot we don't know, and I'd love to see what their lives were like and to fill in some of those gaps.

Do you have any pets?
I don't have any pets, but my family members do, and I visit them all the time! In fact, I love my grandparents' dog Maisy so much that I put her into *Cilla* as Daisy! Maisy is a black

pug, and she loves to sit in my lap and rest her head on my arms while I write.

When did you realize you wanted to be a writer?
I was named "Most Likely to Be a Children's Book Author" in my eighth grade yearbook and wanted to write from that moment on. So that was a pretty impressive yearbook committee!

What do you need with you when you're writing?
I need something to write with (it can be anything: a pen and paper, a computer, or even just my phone!); coffee or green tea; a snack (usually dried seaweed snacks); and of course, chocolate!

What is your writing process like?
I like to say that I "write to think." This means that sometimes, I don't really know what I think about something—an argument, a character, or a story—until I've started writing about it. I write best when I just dive into it; I'm not a big outliner, and even when I plan out my stories, they always seem to change during the writing process!

What is it like to work with an illustrator?
Working with an illustrator is nothing short of amazing! I'm so lucky to have the immensely talented Dana Wulfekotte as my illustrator, and she brings Cilla to life in a way I never could have imagined when I first started writing the series. Working with an illustrator is also really fun. Dana reads an early draft and makes sketches of potential images and scenes. Then, my editor and I look at them and make comments, and Dana uses our comments to create her final drawings. I absolutely love her work, and she very generously sent me some of her original sketches of *Future Author Extraordinaire*.

They're now framed and hanging on my living room wall, so I get to see them (and smile!) every day.

Do you have any writing rituals?
When I'm writing new material, I like to try to do it early in the morning, when I first wake up. This way, I can be really focused—I'm not worrying about the other things I have to do during the day. I also work really well with a timer. I'll usually wake up, get breakfast, light a candle, set a timer, and then write for one hour. This way, no matter what I have to do during the day, I've already had some time to sit with my writing and whatever story I'm working on.

What advice do you have for anyone who wants to be a writer?
Read! Reading is one of the best things you can do if you want to be a writer. By reading and exploring all the different kinds of stories that are out there, you'll learn so much about yourself as a writer: the literary patterns and the kinds of plot twists that intrigue you, the kinds of stories and characters that move you, and the kinds of stories that you *don't* see and would like to. And by read, I don't mean you have to read books that you think are boring but you "should" read. Read whatever makes you happy—from action novels to comics to play scripts!!!

How much of the Cilla Lee-Jenkins series is based on real life?
I've drawn a lot from my own life in writing Cilla, and many of the stories in the Cilla books are based on real events. So, for example, the flower girl scene at the end of *This Book Is a Classic* is based on my cousin Jenn's wedding, when another relative carried the youngest member of our family down the

aisle with a giant flower pinned to her chest. A lot of the characters in Cilla are based on real people, too, or a combination of people. Colleen and Alien-Face McGee are based on a combination of some of my best friends from elementary school through to adulthood. (And in case you were wondering, I *did* make up a story about a friend being an alien in disguise. I didn't call him Alien-Face though: I actually named him "Zorgack the Nerdy." As you can see, I'm sometimes a lot like Cilla.)

Have any of your friends or relatives spotted themselves in your stories? Were they excited to be included?
Yes! For my family especially, reading Cilla has become a "spot the family" game, and hearing their reactions to each new draft—and where they think they see themselves—is such a fun part of the process. My sisters have been especially wonderful about this, and they think it's hilarious that now, at book events, people ask them which one is "The Blob." I have a big family, so my goal is to try to put all my family members into my books someday!

This Book Is a Classic is all about Traditions. What were your favorite family traditions when you were a kid? And do you have any favorite family traditions now?
Like Cilla, I've always loved Traditions, and many of my favorites have made their way into the Cilla books. As a kid, one of my absolute favorite traditions was Chinese New Year; I loved the fireworks, dragon dances, and special foods. Another tradition of ours was going to Dim Sum. My Nai Nai and Ye Ye were very religious, so every Sunday, they'd go to church in Boston Chinatown. My parents and I would always meet them

afterwards, and we'd all go to Dim Sum with them and their church friends, which was such a wonderful tradition and a wonderful way to spend time together. With my other grandparents (who Grandma and Grandpa Jenkins are based on), one of my absolute favorite traditions as a kid was our Passover seders. Passover is a Jewish holiday that's all about traditions: As a family you have a seder, which is a meal where you tell traditional stories and say prayers at the table. There's singing, the best food, and everyone in the family (down to the youngest kids) gets to participate. And of course, on both sides of my family, there were our everyday traditions too: from the mantau and dried pork snacks my Nai Nai and Ye Ye always had ready for me when I came to visit, to the Viennese butter cookies my grandmother and I bake every holiday season!

What do you want readers to remember about your books?
I hope they remember Cilla as a character and something that made them laugh or smile as they read.

What would you do if you ever stopped writing?
I'd be so sad if I ever stopped writing, so I hope that doesn't happen! But if I had to, I'd probably go into something involving children's books and working with kids—like working as a children's librarian.

What is your favorite word?
Persnickety (it's just SO satisfying to say).

If you could live in any fictional world, what would it be?
Harry Potter! One of my favorite coats has two school pins on it—one is my graduate school crest, the other is the Gryffindor crest.

Who is your favorite fictional character?
This is so hard! If I had to pick one, I'd say Rosie from *Maurice Sendak's Really Rosie Starring the Nutshell Kids*.

What was your favorite book when you were a kid? Do you have a favorite book now?
As a kid, *The Lion, the Witch, and the Wardrobe* was my all-time favorite, followed by The Animorphs series by K. A. Applegate. Now my favorites include *The Earthsea Quartet* by Ursula K. Le Guin, *American Born Chinese* by Gene Luen Yang, and *War and Peace* by Leo Tolstoy.

What book is on your nightstand now?
This question is hilariously hard because I have a lot of books in my "to read" pile and technically they're not on my nightstand—I always end up with a pile of books in bed next to me! Right now, I'm loving *Jasmine Toguchi, Flamingo Keeper* by Debbi Michiko Florence, *Front Desk* by Kelly Yang, and *Aru Shah and the End of Time* by Roshani Chokshi.

What would your readers be most surprised to learn about you?
A lot of readers are surprised to learn that I wrote most of the first Cilla book on my phone and on my iPad, at night, in bed! I was in graduate school when I wrote *Cilla*, which meant my days were full with studying and other jobs. So, I snatched the time I had left—on the bus on my way to work and in bed before I fell asleep—to write. Even now that I have more time to write, I still do a lot of writing on my phone when I'm on the subway on my way to work (it probably looks like I'm playing a really intense game!).

Now that Cilla Lee-Jenkins has written a bestseller and a classic, she's going to tackle an epic! Epics are all about struggles, and Cilla is facing her biggest challenge of all time: Her grandfather is recovering from a stroke and has forgotten all his English. Cilla vows to teach him English, while navigating fifth grade, younger siblings, and BOYS!

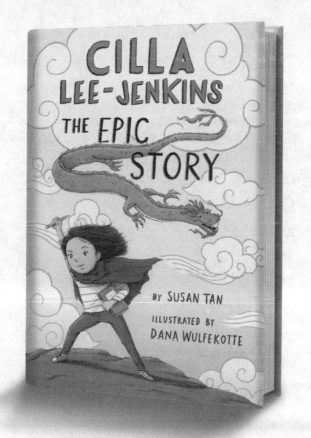

Keep reading for an excerpt!

AN (EPIC) START

Let me tell you, oh reader, of Cilla Lee-Jenkins.
Future author, destiny great.
Her fate in middle school will hopefully be an
    excellent one,
And everyone will like her, and will be impressed
    by how grown-up she is.
The end.

Hi. That kind of beginning—with fancy
language, and almost poetry, and saying
"oh" when you talk to someone—is how you
start an Epic.

Which is what this book is.

An Epic, as you can maybe tell from the word, is a REALLY exciting kind of story, all about Adventure and Fate. Epics have lots of Drama (which I love). They involve some sort of Quest, and usually there are Struggles to overcome, or an enemy to vanquish. Epic heroes perform Feats, like defeating (or making friends with) dragons, or saving the world.

The best part about deciding to write an Epic is that there are so many different kinds. Some Epics are about ancient times and involve traveling on stormy seas, and fighting with swords, and wrestling bears, and whatever else people used to do back then. Other Epics, though, are set in space and involve giant laser beam battles and evil alien slugs. Even lots of superhero books are Epics (especially when a hero has to save the world from being blown up, or turned to molten lava, which happens a lot in superhero stories).

My Epic probably won't have bears or dragons, which is too bad. But it will be about something just as scary. Because this is the Epic story of my last year in elementary school.

It all began on the first day of fifth grade, when Ms. Paradise gave us each a packet of forms to take home to our parents. Right on top was a Very

Official-Looking, Serious letter. It wasn't the exciting kind, with a message telling me I'm about to inherit magical powers and need to go fulfill my destiny, like in the books.

But a letter about middle school.

And how I need to start getting ready for it.

I'm a little (or a lot) nervous about middle school. It's much bigger than my school now, and there are older kids there. Instead of having one classroom I'll have a different one for every subject, with a different teacher, too (which seems excessive). And apparently there will be a lot of Expectations. Expectations about knowing all the times tables, and having total Focus in class, and, worst of all, being Serious and grown-up ALL THE TIME.

Everyone seems to be excited about middle school, not nervous like me. Even Colleen (my best friend!) is happy to go and says things like "I can't wait!" or "One more year!" So I don't know how to tell her that I CAN wait. In fact, I'm happy to wait a long time.

All this could make for a very hard year. But don't worry. Luckily, I'm not just any fifth grader.

I'm destined for greatness as a future author extraordinaire.

I know how to take destiny into my own hands.

Because the most important thing about an Epic is that there is *always* a happy ending. No matter how much you Struggle, if you're in one, you know you'll emerge victorious. By the end you'll have won the treasure, or become queen of a kingdom, or made a new dragon friend. And afterward, everyone will know about your victories and say, "Wow, she's so amazing and mature!" when you pass by.

Which would be wonderful.

Even though my Epic will be a little different because I get seasick on boat rides, am scared of slugs, and don't have superpowers (unfortunately), I know it will still end in the same way.

And when my Epic is done, I should be ready to be a middle schooler.

This book won't just be about overcoming Epic Struggles, though. There will be Adventures, too, and I have TONS to tell you because last year, I didn't write a book at all. So you have lots to look forward to, and I'll introduce you to my friends, and family, and favorite new stories. And, of course, you'll also meet the Foes in my life (they're very important for an Epic, especially when it comes to defeating them).